My Weird School Special

Deck the Halls, We're Off the Walls!

Dan Gutman

Pictures by
Jim Paillot

HARPER
An Imprint of HarperCollinsPublishers

To my Facebook fans

My Weird School Special: Deck the Halls, We're Off the Walls!
Text copyright © 2013 by Dan Gutman
Illustrations copyright © 2013 by Jim Paillot
All rights reserved. Printed in the United States of America.
No part of this book may be used or reproduced in any manner whatsoever without written permission except in the case of brief quotations embodied in critical articles and reviews. For information address HarperCollins Children's Books, a division of HarperCollins Publishers, 10 East 53rd Street, New York, NY 10022.
www.harpercollinschildrens.com

ISBN 978-0-06-220683-1 (lib. bdg.) — ISBN 978-0-06-220682-4 (pbk.)

Typography by Kate Engbring
21 22 23   BRR   20 19 18 17 16 15 14
❖

First Edition

Contents

The Best Christmas Vacation!

My name is A.J., and I hate it when a song gets stuck in my head.

Does that ever happen to you? You hear a song a couple of times and learn the words without even trying. Then you find yourself singing it *all* the time. You sing it while you're walking to school. You sing it while you're taking a bath. You can't stop singing it no matter where you are.

I *hate* when that happens!

Ever since Thanksgiving they've been playing this rap song on the radio over and over again. I can't get it out of my head.

The song is by this kid who isn't much older than me. His name is Johnny Cray, but his rap name is Cray-Z. My sister loves him. Every girl in the *world* loves him.

The song is called "The Christmas Klepto." It's about this mean guy who steals toys. It starts like this. . . .

'Twas the night before Christmas.
You know the rest.
Stuff was all over; the house was all messed.

I was dreaming of a Christmas white.
It was a totally silent night.

That's when I heard a crash and a boom,
So I ran right down to the living room.

There was this guy dressed all in black,
And over his shoulder he carried a sack.

I took one look at him and said, "Whoa, man!
I know you're not Frosty the Snowman."

"Who are you?" I asked after a pause.
"You sure don't look like Santa Claus."

He said, "The name's Klepto. I'm from
the South Pole.
I grab all your presents. That's how I roll.

"On Christmas Eve, I go around the world
and steal all the presents from boys and
girls."

Ugh. That song is the worst part about
Christmas. And now it's stuck in my head
forever.

Do you know what's the *best* part about Christmas? No school for nine whole days! That's right. No homework. No reading, writing, math, or social studies. No teachers.

Yippee!

Nine days! Do you know how long nine days is? I figured it out on my calculator. Nine days is the same as 216 hours. 216 hours is the same as 12,960 minutes. 12,960 minutes is the same as 777,600 seconds. That's a *long* time.

For 777,600 seconds I won't have to see Andrea Young, this annoying girl in my class with curly brown hair.

I'm going to enjoy every one of those seconds. This is going to be the greatest Christmas vacation of my life.

The First Rule of Being a Kid

I was eating breakfast when the greatest Christmas vacation of my life got even *greater.* My mom was sitting at the table reading her newspaper when I saw this on the back page. . . .

SANTA CLAUS IS COMING TO TOWN!

I leaned forward so I could read the small letters. They said that Santa was going to be at our local shopping mall on Saturday, just before Christmas.

All my dreams had come true!

If you ask me, Santa Claus is the greatest

man in the history of the world. Anybody who gives toys to kids should get the No Bell Prize. But I figure Santa will never get the No Bell Prize, because that's a prize they give out to people who don't have bells. And if there's one thing Santa has plenty of, it's bells.

"Can you take me to the mall on Saturday?" I asked my mom. "Please, please, *please*?"

"Dad and I need to clean out the garage on Saturday," my mom replied.

"You can clean out the garage *anytime*, Mom," I told her. "Santa is only going to be at the mall on Saturday. If I don't go, I'll never get to see him for the rest of my *life*."

"Sorry, A.J. Not this Saturday."

"But I need to buy a present for Amy," I begged.

My sister, Amy, is three years older than me. She's annoying, but I have to get her a present anyway.

"No," Mom said. "No means *no*."

Hmmm. Begging usually works for me. I would have to try something else. If at first you don't succeed, try, try again. That's what my parents always say. You can accomplish *anything* if you put your mind to it.

It was time to put Plan B into effect.

I started crying.

If you want something really badly and

the situation is hopeless, there's only one thing to do—cry. That's the first rule of being a kid.

I peeked to see if my mom was watching me cry.

"A.J.," she said. "Those are crocodile tears."

What do crocodiles have to do with anything?

"Come on, Mom!" I pleaded. "I've been waiting to meet Santa Claus my whole life."

Mom put down her newspaper and looked at me. She had a serious look on her face.

"Your father and I have been meaning to tell you something for a while now, A.J.,"

she said. "It's about Santa Claus. We think it's time you knew that Santa—"

But she didn't get the chance to finish her sentence because the phone rang. I picked it up.

It was my friend Ryan, who will eat anything, even stuff that isn't food.

"Santa is coming to the mall!" Ryan

shouted into the phone.

"I know!" I shouted back. "Do you think it's the *real* Santa? I mean, how could he visit every mall in the world?"

"He's not visiting every mall in the world," Ryan told me. "He's just visiting *our* mall! That's why we have to be there. Are you in? My mom said she would drive us. Spread the word."

I hung up and called my friends Michael, Neil, and Alexia to tell them the big news about Santa.

"I want to go!" said Michael, who never ties his shoes.

"I want to go!" said Neil, who we call the nude kid even though he wears clothes.

"I want to go!" said Alexia, who rides a skateboard all the time.

In case you were wondering, everybody was saying they wanted to go.

I looked at my mom with my best puppy dog eyes. If you ever want something really badly, look at your parents with puppy dog eyes. That's the first rule of being a kid.

"Please?" I asked. "Ryan's mom said she'd drive us to the mall. You don't even have to go."

"You'll buy a present for your sister while you're there?" Mom asked.

"Of course!"

"Okay," my mom agreed. "You can go."

Yippee!

A Christmas Miracle

I had to wait a million hundred hours for Saturday to arrive. Wednesday felt like it was two days long. Thursday must have been three days long. Friday took at least a week. I thought I was gonna die of old age.

But finally, it was Saturday. My mom

made me wear the dorky red-and-green Christmas sweater that my aunt knitted for me last year. Ugh, it's itchy.

"Do I *have* to wear this?" I asked.

"Yes," my mom replied. "You want to look your best in front of Santa."

"I don't want to look like a dork in front of Santa," I said.

"You look very handsome, A.J."

When I came downstairs, my sister, Amy, was watching TV in the living room.

"Nice sweater, dork," she told me.

I didn't care what Amy said. It would be worth it to wear a dorky, itchy sweater if I could see Santa Claus live and in person.

I sat in the window for a million hundred minutes waiting for my ride. Finally, Ryan's minivan pulled up.* Ryan, Michael,

---

* I think it's called a minivan because it was invented by some lady named Minnie.

16

Neil, and Alexia were inside. They were all wearing their itchy Christmas sweaters.

"Nice sweaters, dorks," I said as I climbed in.

Lots of people had decorated their front yards for Christmas. We drove past

giant inflatable snowmen, candy canes, Santas, sleighs, and lots of reindeer. It was beautiful. Ryan's mom started to sing *"I'm dreaming of a white Christmas . . ."* and we all joined in.

That's when the most amazing thing in the history of the world happened.

It started to snow!

Well, that may not be all that amazing to *you*. But we live in California, and it hardly *ever* snows here.

"It's snowing!" we all marveled as we pressed our noses against the windows.

It was a Christmas miracle.

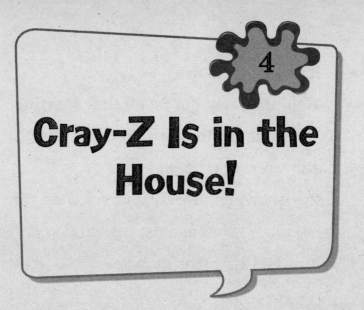

Cray-Z Is in the House!

When we got to the mall, the parking lot was jammed. Ryan's mom circled around trying to find a spot.

"Everybody must be here to see Santa," she said.

"I wonder where he parked his sleigh," Michael said, looking around.

"Santa doesn't park his sleigh in a parking lot, dumbhead," said Neil the nude kid. "That would be *crazy*."

"Where do you think he parked it?" asked Alexia.

"Up on the roof, of course," said Neil.

Right next to the mall entrance was a big bus. On the side of bus, in big red letters, it said: CHRISTMAS RAPPIN' WITH CRAY-Z.

"Cray-Z is here!" shouted Alexia. "That must be his tour bus!"

"Cray-Z?" asked Ryan's mom. "Who's Cray-Z?"

Ryan's mom is really old, so she doesn't know anything. We had to tell her that

Cray-Z is this kid rapper, and his song "The Christmas Klepto" is on the radio all the time.

"Do you like his music?" Ryan's mom asked us.

"Ugh, no!" said Ryan.

"That kid is horrible," said Michael.

"I call him Justin Timberfake," said Neil.

We all said how much we couldn't stand Cray-Z's music. I didn't tell anyone that Cray-Z's dumb song had been stuck in my head all week.

Suddenly, a bunch of girls came running out of the mall. They surrounded the bus.

"We love Cray-Z!" they were shouting. "Marry me, Cray-Z!"

Those girls were screaming and crying

and fainting all over the place. What is their problem?

"Girls are weird," said Alexia, who is technically a girl but likes cool boy stuff anyway.

Finally, Ryan's mom found a parking spot. We had to walk a million hundred miles to get to the entrance of the mall.

"WOW!" we all said, which is "MOM" upside down.

When we walked through the door,

everything was *Christmas-y*. There were candy canes, wreaths, colored lights, jingle bells, and huge paper snowflakes all over the place. **MEET SANTA TODAY** said a banner on the wall. I could hear "Rudolph the Red Nosed Reindeer" playing. Big Christmas ornaments were hanging from the upper level of the mall. Zillions of people were walking around. There was electricity in the air!

Well, not really. If there was electricity in the air, we would get electrocuted.

"You're big kids now," Ryan's mom told us as she took a cell phone out of her pocketbook. "I'm going to do some Christmas shopping. We can stay in touch by phone."

She gave Ryan the cell phone and told him to put it in his pocket.

Cell phones are cool. My mom said I could get one when I'm in high school.

"We'll meet at the food court in two

hours," Ryan's mom told us. "I need you kids to stay together and be careful. Don't get into trouble, do you hear me?"

"*Us* get into trouble?" I asked.

"What could possibly happen?" asked Alexia.

"We *never* get into trouble," said Michael.

Ryan's mom looked at us with those crazy grown-up eyes that make it seem like she's drilling an invisible hole in your head. Then she left.

The mall is big. Right in the middle is a *ginormous* Christmas tree that almost reaches the ceiling. How they got that tree in the mall, I'll never know.

We walked all over the place looking for Santa.

"I'm glad Andrea and Emily aren't here," said Alexia. "They're so annoying."

"Hey, I have an idea," I said. "Let's use Ryan's cell phone and make a prank call to Andrea's house."

Everybody agreed that was a genius idea, so I should make the call. Ryan speed-dialed the number for Andrea's house.

"Hello?" somebody answered.

I wasn't sure if it was Andrea or her mother.

"I would like to order a large pepperoni pizza," I said.

"You must have the wrong number. This is not a pizza parlor."

The gang was cracking up. It was

27

definitely Andrea's mother on the phone.

"Do you have ravioli?" I asked.

"No!"

"How about spaghetti?"

"No!" Andrea's mother said. "Wait a minute. Is this A.J.? Are you calling for Andrea? She's not home. She's at the—"

I didn't hear the end of the sentence, because that's when the most amazing thing in the history of the world happened.

Somebody tapped me on the shoulder. But I'm not going to tell you who it was.

Okay, okay, I'll tell you. But you have to read the next chapter. So nah-nah-nah boo-boo on you.

True Love

5

"Hi Arlo!"

"Ahhhhhhhhhhhhhhh!"

It was Andrea! She's the only person in the world who calls me by my real name.*

I must have jumped three feet in the air. Little Miss Perfect was with her crybaby

---

* Because she knows I don't like it.

friend Emily. They were carrying a bunch of packages.

"What are *you* doing here?" I asked Andrea. "Buying yourself a new encyclopedia because your old one wore out?"

"Very funny," said Andrea. "Emily and I bought toys for homeless girls and boys."

"That's right," said Emily, who always agrees with everything Andrea says. "We want to bring peace and harmony to kids all over the world."

"Oh, yeah? Well, we came to meet Santa Claus," Alexia said.

"Oooooo!" Andrea said, all excited. "We want to meet Santa, *too*. Can we come with you guys?"

"We'll have to talk it over," I said.

The gang and I moved off to the side and huddled up like football players.

"What do you think?" asked Neil. "Should we let them hang out with us?"

"I say no," I said. "I don't want to walk around with Andrea all day."

"Oooooo, A.J. doesn't want to walk with

31

Andrea," said Ryan. "They must be in *love*!"

"Wait a minute!" I yelled. "I told you I *didn't* want to walk with Andrea. Why are you saying I'm in love with her?"

"A.J., everybody knows you love Andrea," said Neil. "It's totally obvious that you only said you didn't want to walk with her to hide the fact that you're in love with her."

Hmmmmm.

"Okay," I said, "in that case, it's okay with me if Andrea walks with us."

"*Oooooo*, A.J. wants to walk with Andrea!" said Ryan. "They must be in *love*!"

"Wait a minute! That's not fair!" I shouted. "So it doesn't matter *what* I say. I'm in love with Andrea whether I want to walk with her or not."

"*Oooooo*, A.J. just admitted he's in love with Andrea!" said Alexia.

"When are you gonna get married?" asked Neil.

If these kids weren't my best friends, I would hate them.

6

Waiting in Line Stinks

Andrea said she knew where Santa was, and she led us to the other side of the mall. Finally, we found the end of the line of people waiting to meet Santa. There must have been a million hundred kids there! I could see a sign in the distance that said **SANTA'S WORKSHOP**, but Santa Claus was too far away. He was in a special roped-off area.

"We should sneak up to the front of the line," I whispered.

"That would be wrong, Arlo," Andrea said. "These kids got here before we did."

I was going to sneak up anyway, but a big arm came down in front of my face. I looked up. You'll never believe whose arm it was.

Officer Spence, our school security guard! He was standing on a Segway. Those things are cool.

"Officer Spence!" I said. "What are *you* doing here?"

"Making sure everybody waits in line,"

he told me. "And earning a little extra money over the holidays."

"How long will we have to wait in line?" Ryan asked.

"About an hour," Officer Spence said.

"An *hour*?!"

"We could die from old age while we're waiting," I said.

"An hour is like forever,"

said Michael.

Andrea rolled her eyes. "Boys should learn to be patient," she said.

I wasn't sure if it was worth it to wait in line for an hour. I thought that maybe we should just forget about meeting Santa. But that's when I heard these magic words. . . .

"Santa is giving out candy," some kid said.

"Santa is giving out candy,"

said some other kid.

"Santa is giving out candy!" said another kid.

In case you were wondering, everybody was saying that Santa was giving out candy. And if there's one thing that I love almost as much as Santa, it's *candy*. All the candy I got on Halloween was gone.

So we decided to stay in line.

But waiting in lines is boring. To kill the time, I practiced what I was going to say when I got to Santa. . . .

"I want the new Striker Smith Commando action figure with missile launcher, voice activator, attack dog, and deluxe blowtorch. Other accessories sold separately. Batteries not included."

Striker Smith is a superhero from the future who travels through time and fights all who dare to thwart his destiny. He can turn into a jet plane when you push a button on his stomach. His armor suit is tough enough to withstand a nuclear blast. He's a one-man wrecking machine, ready to take on any evil to save the world.

Two Christmases ago, I got my first Striker Smith action figure. Then on the school bus I tied a string to Striker's leg and lowered him out the window so he could fight bad guys who were attacking the bus. But Striker fell under the bus and got decapitated. That's a fancy way of saying his head came off. We had a funeral for his head.*

I got a *new* Striker Smith last Christmas. But he met his untimely end when his head got tragically melted in a battle

---

* I wrote this poem in his honor: *Ashes to ashes, dust to dusted. / We buried Striker because he was busted. / He was cool, but now he's dead. / It's hard to live without a head.*

with an evil magnifying glass. So now I wanted to get a new Striker, the one that comes with a blowtorch. It is cool.

Most of the other kids in line were little. They didn't even look like they were in first grade yet. Man, I thought, those kids can't even *read*. They don't know what two plus two equals! They don't know *anything*. It's hard to believe that I was that dumb just a few years ago.

Standing still is the most boring thing in the history of the world. What a snoozefest. The line inched forward a little. I could almost see Santa.

"I bet it's not the *real* Santa," I told Alexia. "It's just some guy in a Santa suit."

The little kid in front of me heard that

and turned around. He was holding his mother's hand, and he looked like he was going to cry. He must have been waiting for a long time already. If these kids didn't get to meet Santa soon, they were going to freak out.

A group of grown-ups strolled by the line singing Christmas carols. Somebody else walked by with a real reindeer. There were more reindeer in a petting zoo.

"Where do you think they got those reindeer?" Michael asked me.

"From Rent-A-Reindeer," I told him. "You can rent anything."

Some lady came by asking kids if they wanted to write a letter to Santa and have it delivered to the North Pole. That was a dumb idea. Santa was right here at the mall. Why would I want to send a letter all the way to the North Pole?

"When are we going to get there?" asked Ryan.

"Waiting in line stinks," I said.

"You boys are annoying," Andrea said. "Why don't you go take a walk? Emily and I will hold your place in line."

She didn't have to ask us twice. We got out of there.

A Present for My Sister

"Let's go to Candy Castle!" Ryan shouted as soon as we got out of the line.

"Let's go to Cinnabon," shouted Michael.

"Let's get ice cream!" said Neil the nude kid.

"Let's go to the skateboard shop!" said Alexia.

Malls are cool. There's so much stuff to see and do, especially around Christmastime. Our mall even has a *train* in it.

We ran over to the train. It goes around and around in circles on metal tracks. At the ticket booth was an elf with a funny hat and pointy ears, like on *Star Trek*. The elf turned around, and you'll never believe who it was.

Mrs. Kormel, our bus driver!

"Mrs. Kormel!" I shouted. "What are *you* doing here?"

"Bingle boo!" she said. "I'm running the train . . . and earning a little extra money over the holidays."

"Aren't you a little tall to be an elf?" asked Alexia.

"Elves come in all sizes," Mrs. Kormel told us. "All aboard! *Toot toot!*"

That train ride looked lame, so we didn't get on. Any train that needs an elf to toot for it must be lame.

We ran over to the escalator. Escalators are cooler than trains, and you don't need tickets to ride them. My friend Billy, who lives around the corner, told me that if you run down an up escalator for ten seconds, you'll travel back in time.*

Neil said he had to go to the bathroom, so we went over to the men's room and waited for him to finish. That's when I remembered that my mom gave me money to buy a present for my sister. I didn't know what to get her. What do you get for an annoying sister?

"You're a girl," I said to Alexia. "What do *you* think my sister would like? Perfume? Jewelry?"

---

* That works with revolving doors, too.

47

"Why don't you get her a new skateboard?" suggested Alexia. "That's what I want."

A *skateboard*!

"My sister doesn't even know how to ride a skateboard," I told Alexia. "Why would she want that?"

"No, that's a *great* idea, A.J.!" said Ryan. "Buy your sister a skateboard. Then when she doesn't use it, the skateboard is yours."

"That's *genius*!" I said.

Alexia and Ryan should be in the gifted and talented program.

Neil came out of the bathroom. We were about to go over to the skateboard shop to buy my sister's present when the most amazing thing in the history of the world happened.

It started with a noise—a high-pitched *screech*. At first it was far away. Then it got louder.

And louder.

There was the thunder of feet. They were getting closer.

And closer.

Then there was screaming!

Then we saw a bunch of girls running in our direction. There must have been five hundred of them.

"EEEEEEEEK!" one of them screamed. "I think I see Cray-Z!"

"I love you, Cray-Z!"

Cray-Z was running right at us, and he was being chased by a thundering herd of screaming girls.

"In here!" I yelled to him. "Follow me!"

Ryan, Michael, Neil, and Alexia formed a human wall to stop the girls. I hustled Cray-Z into the men's bathroom. He was gasping for breath. I thought he was gonna die.

He put his hand on my shoulder and looked me in the eye.

"You gotta help me, dude," he said. "Those girls are *nuts*!"

Plenty of Cray-Z to Go Around

The famous Cray-Z was standing right next to me, live and in person!

"I can't take it anymore!" Cray-Z moaned. "They're gonna tear me apart! I need somewhere to hide!"

I didn't know what to say. I didn't know what to do. I had to think fast.

So I did the first thing that came to my mind.

I took off my pants.

"Quick!" I said to Cray-Z. "Let's switch clothes! They'll never know the difference!"

"Good idea!" Cray-Z said, taking off his pants.

I tore off my itchy Christmas sweater and gave it to Cray-Z. He tore off his clothes and gave them to me. I put on his clothes and he put on mine. I looked pretty sharp with his hat and sunglasses. It was hilarious.

"Do I look like you?" I asked him.

"Yeah," he said. "Do I look like *you*?"

"Yeah," I said. "You chill in here for a while. I'll take care of your fans for you."

I pulled the hat down low over my

face, strolled out of the men's room, and gave a big wave to the girls. They started screaming and pulling out cameras to take my picture.

"Look, it's him! It's Cray-Z!"

"I love you!"

"Can I have your autograph?"

Those girls were totally buying it! They really thought I was Cray-Z!

"Sure you can have my autograph," I said.

The girls started sticking pens and paper in my face. I wrote CRAY-Z as fast as my hand could move.

"One at a time, girls," I said cheerfully. "One at a time. There's plenty of Cray-Z to go around."

"EEEEEEK! I touched him!" a little girl screamed. "I'll never wash this hand again!"

After they got my autograph, girls were fainting, crying, and freaking out all over the place. They didn't know that I was just a regular kid. They had no idea that the *real* Cray-Z was hiding in the bathroom.

It was cool to be a famous celebrity. This

was the greatest day of my life!

But you'll never believe who rolled over on his Segway at that moment.

It was Officer Spence, the mall security guard!

Uh-oh. The jig was up. I figured I was in *big* trouble.

"I'm sorry, Mr. Z," said Officer Spence, "but it's time."

"Time for what?" I asked.

"Time for you to sing."

"Huh? What? M-me?" I stammered. "Nobody told me—"

"Hurry up!" Officer Spence said. "They're all waiting for you."

"Who all? Huh? Where?"

Officer Spence grabbed my hand and pulled me up on his Segway. We rolled over to a stage that had been set up near the center of the mall. There were four musicians on the stage wearing Santa hats.

"Get up there!" yelled Officer Spence.

I climbed up on the stage.

"Yo, Z," said the guitar player. "You the *man*."

The girls started screaming. I looked

out at the sea of faces. Some of these fans were younger than me. Some of them were older than me. A few of them looked like my grandma! That was weird. I gave a little wave, and they all started freaking out like they never saw a guy wave before. A guy in a jacket and tie climbed onto the stage and picked up the microphone.

"Okay, boys and girls," he said. "This is the moment you've all been waiting for. Here's the latest pop sensation to sing 'The Christmas Klepto,' his new hit song . . . *Craaaaaaaaaaay-Zeeeee!*"

The girls screamed even louder. The musicians started playing that annoying song. I had no choice. I grabbed the mic and started rapping. . . .

"'Twas the night before Christmas.
You know the rest.
Stuff was all over; the house was all messed.

I was dreaming of a Christmas white.
It was a totally silent night.

That's when I heard a crash and a boom,
So I ran right down to the living room.

There was this guy dressed all in black,
And over his shoulder he carried a sack.

I took one look at him and said, 'Whoa, man!
I know you're not Frosty the Snowman.'

'Who are you?' I asked after a pause.
'You sure don't look like Santa Claus.'

He said, 'The name's Klepto. I'm from the
South Pole.
I grab all your presents. That's how I roll.

'On Christmas Eve I go around the world
and steal all the presents from boys and girls.'"

You know what? Those girls were digging it! You should have *been* there! The best part was, they were screaming so loud that nobody could tell I wasn't the real Cray-Z. So I kept rapping. . . .

"He went to the corner and got down
on one knee
To scoop up the gifts that were under
our tree.

He took them all. He grabbed my new
toys.
He took my new clothes. He took all
our joy.
To the Christmas Klepto, everything's free.
'I'll take your partridge,' he said, 'and
your pear tree.

I like your presents, and now they're mine.
Say, how much of this stuff did you buy
online?

60

'You better watch out. You better not cry.
You make one peep, and I'll poke out
your eye.'

'You're a mean man, sir!' I said with a hiss.
Just wait until Santa finds out about this.'"

I didn't get to finish the song because that guy in the jacket and tie hopped up on the stage again and grabbed the mic away from me.

"Isn't Cray-Z fantastic?" he yelled. "He'll be back at two o'clock to sing for you some more."

The girls screamed. Officer Spence grabbed my hand. I hopped on his

Segway, and he took me back to the men's bathroom.

In the bathroom, Cray-Z was looking in the mirror and combing his hair. When he saw me, he turned around and gave me a hug.

"You saved my life, dude!" he told me. "I owe you one, big-time."

Take a Chill Pill

When I came out of the bathroom wearing my regular clothes, the whole gang clapped me on the back.

"You were *awesome*, A.J.!" said Alexia.

"Those girls didn't suspect a thing," said Ryan.

"How did you know the words to that dumb song?" asked Michael.

"It's been stuck in my head all week!" I admitted.

We hustled through the crowd to get back to Santa's Workshop, all the way at the other end of the mall. It took a long time to find Andrea and Emily. They were close to the front of the line now.

"Where *were* you?" Andrea asked with her mean face on. "What took you so long?"

"It's almost our turn to meet Santa!" said Emily.

"Take a chill pill," I told them. "We're here, right?"

I could see Santa Claus now. He was sitting on this big throne with his red suit, red hat, white beard, and black boots—the whole getup. Santa was fat and jolly, just like I imagined. He was surrounded by Christmas trees, presents, fake snow, and a giant nutcracker on each side.*

"Ho! Ho! Ho!" Santa bellowed.

"Y'know, I'm not sure that's the real Santa," said Neil the nude kid.

"It looks like Santa to me," said Michael.

"I'm so excited!" said Andrea, rubbing her hands together.

Soon it would be our turn. We were on

---

* Man, there must be some big nuts if they need such big nutcrackers.

pins and needles.

Well, not really. We were just standing there. If we were on pins and needles, it would have hurt.

I got up on my tiptoes to look all around. There were so many happy, smiling faces. Christmas trees. Twinkling lights. Jingle bells jingling. It was a beautiful scene.

"Ah," I said, "I love the smell of tinsel at Christmastime."

"Tinsel doesn't smell, dumbhead," said Andrea. "That's pine needles that you smell."

"It's your *face* that I smell," I said.

Why can't a truck full of tinsel fall on Andrea's head?

Just then, one of Santa's elves came running down the line of kids. "It's almost your turn to meet Santa!" she said.

That's when I realized that the elf wasn't a real elf. It was our librarian, Mrs. Roopy! She was dressed up like an elf!

"Mrs. Roopy!" I said. "What are *you* doing here?"

"Who's Mrs. Roopy?" asked Mrs. Roopy. "I'm one of Santa's helpers from the North Pole."

She wasn't fooling anybody. It was Mrs. Roopy for sure. That's when I realized that *all* of Santa's helpers were grown-ups from our school. The guy playing Christmas songs on the organ was our music teacher, Mr. Loring. The lady dressed up like Frosty the Snowman was our custodian, Miss Lazar. Another one of the elves was our Spanish teacher, Miss Holly.

"Miss Holly!" I said when I saw her. "What are *you* doing here?"

"Earning a little extra money over the holidays," she said. "We all are. *¡Feliz Navidad!*"

"I guess teachers don't get paid very much," said Ryan.

"Teachers get paid?" I asked. "I thought they just came to school every day because they had no place else to go."

There was just one family in front of us in line now. A lady with a big camera came over. I did a double take. The lady was Ms. Hannah, our art teacher!

"Merry Christmas!" she said. "Now listen up. When you sit on Santa's lap, I'm going to snap your picture. So let's see some big smiles, okay?"

"Okay!" we all said.

"Do you want to buy the twenty-dollar package or the forty-dollar package?" Ms. Hannah asked us.

"Package of *what*?" I said.

"Package of pictures, of course," said Ms. Hannah. "The twenty-dollar package includes one eight-by-ten in a nice frame. The forty-dollar package includes *two* framed eight-by-tens and ten wallet-size pictures. I suggest you buy the forty-dollar package so you can share your pictures with your grandparents, your aunts, your uncles. . . ."

What a scam.

"I don't want to buy *any* package," I

told Ms. Hannah.

"Yeah," said Alexia. "We just want to meet Santa."

"Fine," Ms. Hannah said. But she said it in a way that meant "not fine."*

The family in front of us had six annoying kids: three boys and three girls. None of them would sit still. They were all sticking their fingers in Santa's nose, poking him in the eyes, and pulling on his beard. It took like a million hundred hours for Ms. Hannah to take a picture of each of the kids. Then she had to take a picture of just the boys. Then she had to take a picture of just the girls. Then she

---

* Only grown-ups can do that. I guess that's why we go to school—so we can learn how to say one thing and mean the exact opposite thing.

had to take a family picture. I thought I was gonna die from old age.

But finally, the last little whining nerd got up from Santa's lap. It was our turn.

"Okay, which one of you wants to go first?" asked Mrs. Roopy.

"I'm sc-scared of Santa," said Emily, who's scared of everything.

"Me too," said Alexia.

"So am I," said Andrea, Neil, Ryan, and Michael.

I had just sung that dumb rap song in front of a million hundred screaming girls. I wasn't afraid of *anything*.

"I'm not scared," I said. "I'll go first."

This was going to be the greatest moment of my life.

My Turn

I stepped up on the platform where Santa was sitting and climbed on his lap. Ms. Hannah told me to smile, and she snapped my picture.

This was *it*. Everything I had ever done had been leading up to this moment. Now my life was complete. If I suddenly dropped dead, at least I could say that I had met Santa Claus.

That is, if I hadn't dropped dead. Because if you're dead, you can't talk.

"Ho! Ho! Ho!" Santa said as he handed me a candy cane and a coloring book.

Whew! Santa has bad breath!

"Say, little boy, your name isn't A.J. by any chance, is it?"

"How did *you* know?" I asked.

"I'm Santa," Santa said. "I see you when you're sleeping. I know when you're awake."

"That's creepy," I said. "Do you have night vision goggles?"

"Ha! Ha! Ha!" laughed Santa. "No, but I know if you've been bad or good, A.J. Be good for goodness' sake!"

Santa must have a GPS and state-of-the-art surveillance technology. I'm not sure, but I think that's an invasion of privacy.

"So what do you want for Christmas, A.J.?" Santa asked me.

"I want the new Striker Smith

Commando," I said. "It comes with a missile launcher, voice activator, attack dog, and deluxe blowtorch. All other accessories sold separately. Batteries not included."

"Striker Smith?" said Santa. "You mean the superhero action figure from the future who travels through time and fights all who dare to thwart his destiny?"

"Yes!"

Wow, Santa really knows his toys.

"A.J., didn't I bring you a Striker Smith action figure two Christmases ago?" Santa asked me.

"Yeah," I replied. "He fell under the school bus, and his head came off."

"And didn't I bring you *another* Striker

Smith action figure last Christmas?"

"Yeah," I said. "He met his untimely end when his head got tragically melted in a battle with an evil magnifying glass."

"I'm sorry to hear that," Santa said. "I hope you'll take better care of Striker Smith *this* year."

"I will, Santa!"

"Good. Merry Christmas, A.J. Ho! Ho! Ho!"

I looked out at the kids waiting in line. I wondered how Santa would remember which presents we all asked him for.

"Are you going to write down that I asked for a Striker Smith action figure?" I asked Santa.

"That won't be necessary," he replied.

"How will you remember, Santa?"

"My mind is like a steel trap," he told me.

"You catch animals with your head?" I asked.

"No, I mean I have a good memory," Santa told me. "That's how I remember what I bring you each year."

Some of the parents in the crowd were looking at their watches. I guess my time was up. But this might be the only chance in my whole life that I would get to talk with Santa. I didn't want to leave.

"Can I ask you one question, Santa?"

"Sure, A.J."

"I understand how reindeer can fly," I said, "but doesn't your sleigh need a wing on each side, for stability?"

"The Christmas spirit lifts it up," Santa said.

"Yeah, but the sleigh doesn't look very aerodynamic," I told him. "Why not use a helicopter instead?"

"I thought you had just *one* question," Santa said.

"How is it possible to visit every house in the world in one night?" I asked. "What about the houses that don't have chimneys? What about people who live in apartments? How do you fit all the toys in the sleigh? And what do you do the rest of the year?"

"We have to wrap this up, A.J.," said Santa. "There are a lot of children waiting."

"You should really lose some weight," I told him. "Obesity is a big problem these days. Have you checked your cholesterol? Isn't it cold at the North Pole? Is there a supermarket up there? Where do you buy your groceries? Have you considered relocating to a warmer climate? Do the reindeer ever poop on people's heads?"

"Time's up, kid!" one of the parents shouted. "Let's move it along, okay?"

I got up from Santa's lap. But as I was doing that, my itchy Christmas sweater must have got caught on Santa. Because that's when the strangest thing in the history of the world happened.

His beard came off!

The Kid Who Ruined Christmas

"Gasp!" everyone gasped.

"Hey," I said. "You're not the *real* Santa! You're just some guy dressed *up* like Santa!"

"Uh . . . well . . . um . . . ," Santa mumbled.

The fake Santa guy looked really familiar to me. I knew I had seen him somewhere before. So I picked his Santa hat up off his head. And you'll never believe in a million hundred years what was under there.

Nothing!

The guy was completely bald, just like Mr. Klutz, the principal of my school!

In fact, the fake Santa guy *was* Mr. Klutz!

"Mr. Klutz!" I shouted. "What are *you* doing here?"

"Uh . . . earning a little extra money over the holidays," he replied.

I knew I was in trouble as soon as people saw Santa wasn't the real Santa. But I had no idea how much trouble I was in.

"EEEEEEEK!" some girl shouted. "Santa has no hair!"

"He's a fake!" a boy yelled.

"Mommy!" screamed another girl. "You told me that man was the real Santa Claus! You lied!"

All the little kids in line started yelling, screaming, crying, and freaking out. Their parents were upset, too.

"We've been waiting in line for an *hour*," a lady shouted, "and now *this*!"

"It's *that* kid's fault!" one dad yelled,

pointing his finger at me. "He ruined Christmas for my son. He ruined Christmas for *everybody*!"

I thought I was gonna die. Mr. Klutz looked scared. He got up quickly and put a sign on his seat that said **SANTA HAS GONE TO FEED HIS REINDEER. HE'LL BE BACK SOON.**

"I'd better get out of here," he told me.

"A.J., what do you have to say for yourself?"

I didn't know what to say. I didn't know what to do. I had to think fast.

"Uh, peace on earth, goodwill to men?" I said.

"Get him!" somebody shouted. "Get that kid who ruined Christmas!"

Bummer in the winter! There was only one thing I could do.

Run!

The True Meaning of Christmas

This was the worst thing to happen since TV Turnoff Week! I wanted to go to Antarctica and live with the penguins.

I jumped off the little platform to make a run for it, but I slipped on some fake snow and knocked over the Christmas tree. It landed on top of me.

As I was scrambling to get up, my foot

got tangled in a string of Christmas lights. When I yanked at it, sparks started flying.

That must have spooked the reindeer in the petting zoo, because one of them broke out of the gate and started running around in crazy circles.

"Run for your life!" shouted Neil the nude kid. "The reindeer is on the loose!"

"Watch out for those antlers!" a lady screamed.

"It's heading for the food court!" somebody shouted.

I finally got to my feet, and a bunch of angry parents started chasing me.

"Get him!" one of the dads shouted. "Get that kid!"

I bolted out of there. Crowds of people

were all over the place. I had to run around them like a football player to escape the angry parents chasing me. I bumped into some lady, and she fell into a fountain.

"Help!" I shouted. "They're gonna kill me!"

I ran up the down escalator. Then I ran down the up escalator. But I didn't travel through time. The parents were still chasing me. I couldn't lose them!

At the other end of the mall, I spotted the men's bathroom. Maybe I could hide in a stall, I figured. It was my only hope.

I ran over there and ducked inside the bathroom. I was panting and gasping for breath.

And you'll never believe who was in

there, combing his hair in the mirror.

Cray-Z!

"Dude!" he said. "What's the matter? You look like you've been through a war!"

I put my hand on his shoulder and looked him in the eye.

"You've got to help me!" I begged. "I was sitting on Santa's lap, and I accidentally pulled off his beard. The kids who were waiting in line freaked out, and now their parents are trying to get me! What should I do?"

"Quick!" Cray-Z said. "Let's switch clothes again!"

"Huh?"

"Just do it!"

I tore off my itchy Christmas sweater

and gave it to Cray-Z. He tore off his clothes and gave them to me.

"Now get out of here!" Cray-Z said. "And act casual."

I whistled as I strolled out of the bathroom.* A bunch of angry parents were milling around, looking all over. None of them noticed me. I thought I was in the clear.

But that's when the most amazing thing in the history of the world happened. An announcement came over the public address system.

Well, that's not the amazing part, because announcements come over the

---

* Because if you're whistling, nobody thinks you did anything wrong. That's the first rule of being a kid.

public address system all the time. The amazing part was what happened next.

"Attention, shoppers. It's two o'clock. The young pop sensation Cray-Z is about to do some more Christmas rapping on the main stage near the big tree. Come see him perform!"

Suddenly, Officer Spence came rolling over to me on his Segway.

"We've been looking all over for you, Mr. Z!" he said. "Come on! Everybody's waiting!"

"Huh? What? Who? Me? Again?" I asked.

Officer Spence pulled me up on the Segway and rolled over to the stage.

"Yo, Z," said the guitar player. "Let's rock, man."

There must have been a million hundred girls in the audience now. Some of them were trying to climb up on the stage, but the police were holding them back. That guy in the jacket and tie climbed up and took the microphone.

"Okay, boys and girls," he said. "Here he is again. The latest. The greatest . . . *Craaaaaaaaaaaay-Zeeeee!*"

The girls started screaming. The band started playing. I had no choice. So I started rapping. . . .

"'Twas the night before Christmas.
You know the rest.
Stuff was all over; the house was all messed.

I was dreaming of a Christmas white.
It was a totally silent night.

That's when I heard a crash and a boom,
So I ran right down to the living room.

There was this guy dressed all in black,
And over his shoulder he carried a sack.

I took one look at him and said, 'Whoa, man!
I know you're not Frosty the Snowman.'

'Who are you?' I asked after a pause.
'You sure don't look like Santa Claus.'

He said, 'The name's Klepto. I'm from
the South Pole.

I grab all your presents. That's how I roll.

'On Christmas Eve I go around the world
and steal all the presents from boys and girls.'

He went to the corner and got down on
one knee
To scoop up the gifts that were under
our tree.

He took them all. He grabbed my new toys.
He took my new clothes. He took all
our joy.

To the Christmas Klepto, everything's free.
'I'll take your partridge,' he said, 'and
your pear tree.

'I like your presents, and now they're
mine.
Say, how much of this stuff did you buy
online?

'You better watch out. You better not cry.
You make one peep, and I'll poke out
your eye.'

'You're a mean man, sir!' I said with a hiss.
Just wait until Santa finds out about this.'

That Mr. Klepto thought he was a smarty,
But in the end, we spoiled his party.

Oh sure, the guy had lots of charm,
Until he tripped our silent alarm.

A few minutes later, the cops arrived.
Mr. Klepto, under the couch he dived.

The cops yelled, 'Come out with your
hands in the air.'
'I was framed!' he shouted. 'This ain't
fair!'

The cops said, 'Now don't try anything
violent.
All you have is the right to remain silent.'

They dragged him away, and he said,
'Bye-bye.'
And that was the last I heard of that
guy.

Now all this stuff that I've been rappin'
You may say that none of it happened.

After all, nobody came and stole your stuff.
Nobody broke in. Nobody got rough.

Well, the reason that you've got nothing to fear
Is because they put Klepto away for ten years!

So you can believe what you want to believe,
But that's what happened on Christmas Eve."

"Let's hear it for Cray-Z!" said the guy with the jacket and tie.

The girls went nuts, screaming and yelling and freaking out. I jumped off the stage and ran back to the men's room. Cray-Z was in there waiting for me.

"You saved my life," I told him.

"Now we're even, dude."

Cray-Z and I switched back into our normal clothes, shook hands, and said good-bye. As I was about to walk away, I came up with the greatest idea in the history of the world.

"Hey, Cray-Z. I need to get a Christmas present for my sister. Can you give me an autograph?"

"Sure, dude," he said.

Cray-Z took off his hat. He pulled a Sharpie from his pocket, signed the hat, and handed it to me.

"Y'know," he said, "sometimes I wish I was in your shoes."

"Why?" I asked. "What's wrong with *your* shoes?"

"No," he said, "what I mean is that the grass is always greener on the other side."

"Huh?" I asked. "What does the color of grass have to do with anything?"

That Cray-Z kid is weird. Who cares about shoes and grass?

But as I walked away, I started thinking about what Cray-Z said. Christmas isn't about malls and elves and trees and presents. It's about being a good person. It's about helping a guy out when he's in trouble. Cray-Z needed my help, so I helped him. Then I needed *his* help, and he helped me. Christmas is a time for giving. *That's* the true meaning of Christmas spirit.

Who knows? Maybe I'll become Cray-Z's stunt double. Maybe Santa will bring me the new Striker Smith Commando action figure with missile launcher, voice activator, attack dog, and deluxe blowtorch. Maybe another song will get stuck in my head. Maybe the real Santa will come to the mall next Christmas.

Maybe they'll pay the teachers more money so they don't have to dress up like elves. Maybe I'll travel back in time on an escalator. Maybe Santa will get some breath mints. Maybe I won't have to wear my itchy Christmas sweater next year. Maybe I'll get to eat some of those giant nuts. Maybe Santa will be arrested for invading people's privacy. Maybe Mr. Klutz will catch animals with his head. Maybe Santa will ditch his sleigh and switch to a helicopter. Maybe Andrea and Emily will bring peace and harmony to kids all over the world.

But it won't be easy!

DecK the Halls, We're Off the Walls!

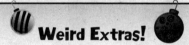 **Weird Extras!**

★ Professor A.J.'s Weird Christmas Facts

★ Fun Games and Weird-Word Puzzles

★ My Weird School Trivia Questions

★ The World of Dan Gutman Checklist

PROFESSOR A. J.'S WEIRD CHRISTMAS FACTS

Howdy, My Weird School fans! Professor A.J. here. I'm gonna tell you a bunch of stuff you probably don't know about Christmas. It's really important for you to learn stuff so you won't grow up to be a dumbhead like a certain person in my class with curly brown hair who rolls her eyes and says mean things to me all the time. But it wouldn't be polite to name names.*

First of all, do you know how the tradition of the Christmas tree got started? It was

---

* Andrea

back in 1897. On Christmas Eve that year, a huge pine tree fell on top of a house in Lake Placid, New York. The Bates family was just sitting down to their Christmas dinner when the tree crashed through their roof and landed in their living room. The family freaked out and were really angry that they would have to spend their Christmas Eve getting that dumb tree out of their living room. So they decided just to leave it there. And ever since that day, people have been putting trees in their living rooms at Christmastime.

Okay, I totally made that story up, so nah-nah-nah boo-boo on you!

But here's some *true* stuff about Christmas. . . .

—The first song to be broadcast from space was "Jingle Bells", on December 16, 1965. The crew of the *Gemini 6* sang the song and played a harmonica.

Most people don't know that the astronauts *wanted* to play the song on a piano, but it wouldn't fit in the space capsule.

FACT:
—Do you know what the word "mistletoe" really means? You better sit down for this one. Mistletoe means "dung on a twig."

That's right! Bird dung! Honest, I did not make that up. You can't make up stuff that good.

FACT:
—You know that character Tiny Tim in Charles Dickens's classic *A Christmas Carol*? Well, before he named the character Tiny Tim, Dickens considered naming the character Puny Pete, Small Sam, or Little Larry.

Ha! I bet that book would have sold a lot more copies if he titled it *Puny Pete Has Nothing to Eat!*

—The coolest shopping mall in the world is the Mall of the Emirates in Dubai. Do you know why? Because it has its own indoor ski slope!

Can you believe that? Dubai is in the desert, so they put in a ski slope. That's weird.

FACT:

—In Columbus, Texas, they have a Santa Claus Museum. There are more than two thousand Santas on display.

The museum even has a Santa doorbell!

FACT:

—Foreign languages are weird. If you wanted to say "Merry Christmas" in Italian, you'd say "*Buon Natale.*" In Spanish it's "*Feliz Navidad.*" In French it's "*Joyeux Noël.*" In German it's "*Frohe Weihnachten.*"

And if you were in outer space and you said "Merry Christmas" to somebody, you would die instantly, because there's no oxygen in outer space.

FACT:

—In Italy they celebrate Christmas on January 6. They call it the Feast of the Epiphany. A witch called La Befana rides on her broomstick the night before and fills kids' stockings with presents if they're good and lumps of coal if they're bad.

That's why I'll never go to Italy over Christmas vacation. First of all, boys have to wear stockings. Not only that, but you might have to walk around in stockings with coal in them. That would hurt!

—Speaking of stockings, kids once used their regular old socks for presents from Santa. That came from an old Dutch tradition in which kids would leave their shoes out with food for Saint Nicholas's donkeys, and he would leave presents in return.

Ugh, disgusting! Dutch people put food in their shoes and let donkeys eat out of them. They're weird.

FACT:
—Did you know that the United States has an official Christmas tree? It's a giant sequoia in California that's over 1,500 years old.

Wow, that's almost as old as my parents.

I could tell you a lot more stuff about Christmas, but I'd rather open my presents and go play out in the snow. Happy holidays!

Professor A.J. (the professor of awesomeness)

FUN GAMES AND WEIRD-WORD PUZZLES

I. WHERE'S SANTA?

Directions: Santa needs to deliver his gifts, but he doesn't want to be seen! Can you find where he is hidden in this picture?

2. WINTER WORD JUMBLE

Directions: The eight words below are all jumbled up! Can you put the letters in correct order and uncover the holiday words?

1. PNSRETE: _____

2. YJO: _____

3. WOSMNAN: _____

4. SBLLE: _____

5. EGIHLS: _____

6. SCHNETTSU: _____

7. CNRAUERTKC: _____

8. DRNEIREE: _____

3. GIFT GIVER

Directions: Everyone has something special they want for Christmas. Match these weird people and animals below with the gift that they would most want from Santa!

4. SNOWFLAKE MATCH

Directions: Snowflakes are falling! Each snowflake is an identical match with another snowflake on the page. Can you find all the matches?

5. CRAZY-CHRISTMAS WORD SEARCH

Directions: Can you find all ten Christmas words that are hidden in this messy jumble of letters?

```
E K A L F W O N S E F U V S M
M O E Z V L X Q I V L D X I W
Q X C L H X D Y W L D F S K M
U M A F O Q S X W F O T X I P
C D N G H P E W J F L W T H X
R W D K C L H K X E D A P T I
K Y Y I X H Z T T M R K A S U
B C C A X J R O R E D C G T X
X V A H J F E I T O G G C N R
B L N B H X B N S W N B I E Y
B C E N T U I W Q T H N S S G
I F Q Y H W O F J L M R B E M
J I N G L E B E L L S A M R V
A N G E L D W W P Q M W S P A
Y S U N Z M F I P S R X K A P
```

**ANGEL CHRISTMAS ELF JINGLE BELLS
MISTLETOE CANDY CANE NORTH POLE
PRESENTS SNOWFLAKE WINTER**

6. ORNAMENT OOPS

Directions: The ornaments on this Christmas tree all spell special holiday words, but it seems that a few have gone missing! Can you figure out the missing letters in each of these words? After you've found all of the letters, put them in order on the lines below the tree to reveal the answer to the mystery question!

___ E R ___ Y

___ T O ___ K I N G

H O ___ I D ___ Y

S ___ G A R P L U M ___

Who Is Santa's Favorite Helper?

___ ___ ___. ___ ___ ___ ___ ___

MY WEIRD SCHOOL TRIVIA QUESTIONS

There's no way in a million hundred years you'll get all these answers right. So nah-nah-nah boo-boo on you!

Q: WHAT IS A.J.'S SISTER'S NAME?
A: Amy

Q: WHICH STAFF MEMBER INVENTED A SECRET LANGUAGE THAT MAKES NO SENSE?
A: Mrs. Kormel

Q: WHAT IS MS. HANNAH'S DRESS MADE OF?
A: Pot holders she bought on eBay

Q: WHERE DO THE KIDS EAT LUNCH?
A: In the vomitorium

Q: HOW DID MISS SMALL BREAK HER LEG?
A: She fell out of a tree.

Q: WHAT DOES ANDREA DO EVERY THURSDAY AFTER SCHOOL?
A: Clog dancing

Q: WHAT IS ANDREA'S FAVORITE MOVIE?
A: Annie

Q: WHO DOES A.J. WANT TO MARRY WHEN HE GROWS UP?
A: Mrs. Cooney, the nurse

Q: WHAT DOES YAWYE STAND FOR?
A: You Are What You Eat

Q: WHO IS ELLA MENTRY SCHOOL NAMED AFTER?

A: Ella Mentry

Q: WHAT DOES MISS LAZAR HAVE IN HER SECRET ROOM DOWN IN THE BASEMENT?

A: A museum of toilet-bowl plungers

Q: WHY DOESN'T A.J. HAVE AN INVISIBLE FRIEND ANYMORE?

A: He got into an argument with his invisible friend, so they stopped being friends.

Q: WHAT FUEL POWERS MR. DOCKER'S CAR?

A: Potatoes

Q: WHAT IS BRAINWASHING?

A: That's when bald guys shampoo their head

Q: WHAT IS A.J.'S FAVORITE HOLIDAY?

A: Take Our Daughters to Work Day, because Andrea is absent from school

Q: WHY IS PRESIDENT'S DAY SPECIAL, ACCORDING TO MICHAEL?

A: Because that's the day big-screen TVs go on sale

Q: WHY ARE SHOVELS BETTER THAN COMPUTERS?

A: Because you can't dig a hole with a computer

Q: WHAT DOES IT MEAN WHEN TEACHERS MAKES A PEACE SIGN WITH THEIR FINGERS?

A: It means "shut up."

Q: WHY DO YOU CLAP AT THE END OF AN ASSEMBLY?

A: Because you're glad it's over.

Q: HOW DOES MRS. YONKERS POWER HER COMPUTER?

A: She runs on a giant hamster wheel.

Q: WHAT IS SPECIAL ABOUT MRS. YONKERS'S PENCIL SHARPENER?

A: It is remote-controlled.

Q: WHAT IS DR. CARBLES'S FIRST NAME?

A: He wants to be Frank, but his name is Milton.

Q: WHERE DOES MR. KLUTZ GET A PIG?

A: From Rent-A-Pig

ANSWER KEY

WHERE'S SANTA?

WINTER WORD JUMBLE

1. PNSRETE: PRESENT
2. YJO: JOY
3. WOSMNAN: SNOWMAN
4. SBLLE: BELLS
5. EGIHLS: SLEIGH
6. SCHNETTSU: CHESTNUTS
7. CNRAUERTKC: NUTCRACKER
8. DRNEIREE: REINDEER

GIFT GIVER

SNOWFLAKE MATCH

CRAZY-CHRISTMAS
WORD SEARCH

```
E K A L F W O N S E F U V S M
M O E Z V L X Q I V L D X I W
Q X C L H X D Y W L D F S K M
U M A F O Q S X W F O T X I P
C D N G H P E W J F L W T H X
R W D K C L H K X E D A P T I
K Y Y I X H Z T T M R K A S U
B C C A X J R O P E D C G T X
X V A H J F E I T O G G C N R
B L N B H X B N S W N B I E Y
B C E N T U I W Q T H N S S G
I F Q Y H W O F J L M R B E M
J I N G L E B E L L S A M R V
A N G E L D W W P Q M W S P A
Y S U N Z M F I P S R X K A P
```

ORNAMENT OOPS

WHO IS SANTA'S FAVORITE HELPER?

MRS. CLAUS

THE WORLD OF DAN GUTMAN CHECKLIST

MY WEIRD SCHOOL

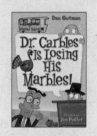

MY WEIRD SCHOOL DAZE

MY WEIRDER SCHOOL

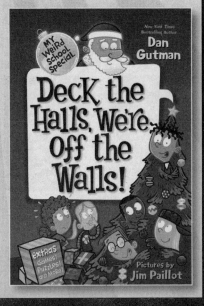

Miss
Holly Is
Too Jolly!

Miss Holly Is Too Jolly!

Dan Gutman

Pictures by

Jim Paillot

HarperTrophy®
An Imprint of HarperCollinsPublishers

Miss Holly Is Too Jolly!

Text copyright © 2006 by Dan Gutman

Illustrations copyright © 2006 by Jim Paillot

All rights reserved. Printed in the United States of America.

No part of this book may be used or reproduced in any manner whatsoever without
written permission except in the case of brief quotations embodied in critical articles
and reviews. For information address HarperCollins Children's Books, a division of
HarperCollins Publishers, 195 Broadway, New York, NY 10007.

Library of Congress Cataloging-in-Publication Data is available.

ISBN-10: 0-06-085382-4 (pbk.) — ISBN-13: 978-0-06-085382-2 (pbk.)

ISBN-10: 0-06-085383-2 (lib. bdg.) — ISBN-13: 978-0-06-085383-9 (lib. bdg.)

❖

First Harper Trophy edition, 2006

Visit us on the World Wide Web!

www.harpercollinschildrens.com

21 BRR 40 39 38 37

To Emma

Contents

Christmas, Hanukkah, and Kwanzaa

"Me llamo A.J. y odio la escuela."

That's "My name is A.J. and I hate school" in Spanish.

Miss Holly translated it for me. She's the Spanish teacher at Ella Mentry School.

"It's not fair," I said as our class walked down the hall to the language lab. "Why do we have to learn a whole nother language?"

"'Nother' isn't a word, Arlo," said Andrea Young. "You can't even speak *English* correctly."

Andrea is this girl in my class with curly brown hair who thinks she knows everything. She calls me by my real name because she knows I hate it.

"'Nother' is *too* a word," I told her.

"Is not."

"Is too."

We went back and forth like that for a while. Andrea said she looked up "nother" in the dictionary once, and it wasn't there. She's probably the only kid in the world who keeps a dictionary on her desk so she can look up words and show everybody how smart she is.

"'*Another*' is a word," Andrea said, "but not 'nother.'"

"Oh yeah?" I said. "If 'nother' isn't a word, then why did you just say it?"

Nah-nah-nah boo-boo on her.

Andrea was wearing this dumb hat that she made all by herself in her knitting class. Andrea takes classes in everything. She probably even takes a class in how to be annoying, because that's the one thing she's good at.

After walking a million hundred miles, we finally got to the language lab. What a dumb name. Labs are supposed to have test tubes and mad scientists and hunch-backed guys named Igor who limp. Our language lab is just a plain old room where we learn Spanish. What's up with that?

"Isn't learning Spanish fun?" Andrea said to her crybaby friend Emily. "I hope Miss Holly teaches us—"

She didn't get the chance to finish her sentence because at that very second Miss Holly danced in the door.

Miss Holly was playing a guitar and she had a big basket of fruit on her head. She was singing some crazy song and spin-ning around and stamping her feet. Her

red dress had pic-
tures of reindeer on
the back. On the front
were blinking lights
and the words "Happy
Holidays!"

When she finished the
song, Miss Holly yelled,
"Olay!" which is the name
of the stuff my mom
smears on her face at night.

"*¡Feliz Navidad!*" Miss Holly said.
"Happy Hanukkah! *Kwanzaa Yenu Iwe
Na Heri!*"

"What the heck does that mean?" I
asked.

5

"That means Merry Christmas, Happy Hanukkah, and Happy Kwanzaa!" Miss Holly replied.

"Which holiday do *you* celebrate?" asked Emily.

"Me?" said Miss Holly. "I celebrate *all* of them!"

If you ask me, it was a little early to be talking about the holidays. I mean, we just came back to school from Thanksgiving break a few days ago. Miss Holly is *too* jolly.

"I love all the holidays!" Miss Holly said. "I can't wait for December!"

"My favorite holiday is Halloween," said Neil, who everybody calls the nude kid, even though he wears clothes.

"My favorite holiday is Thanksgiving," said my friend Ryan, who will eat anything, even stuff that is not food.

"My favorite holiday is my birthday," said my other friend Michael, who never ties his shoes.

Everybody started shouting out their favorite holiday.

"What's *your* favorite holiday, A.J.?" Miss Holly asked me.

"My favorite holiday is Take Our Daughters to Work Day," I said.

"That's for *girls*," Andrea said. "Why is that *your* favorite holiday, Arlo?"

"Because *you're* not here," I replied.

"That's mean!" Andrea said. She crossed her arms and wrinkled up her face.

She was right. It *was* mean. That's why I said it!

I hate her.

Weird Words

"¡*Hola!*" Miss Holly said. "Today we're going to learn Spanish vocabulary words."

"Yay!" said the girls.

"Boo!" said the boys.

"The first word is 'toupee,'" said Miss Holly.

I know what a toupee is. It's fake hair that guys wear so they won't look bald. Our principal, Mr. Klutz, should get one because he's as bald as a bowling ball.

"The Spanish word for 'toupee' is *el peluquín*," said Miss Holly.

"*El peluquín*," we all repeated.

"Good," said Miss Holly. "The next word is 'lifeguard.' The Spanish word for 'lifeguard' is *el salvavidas*."

"*El salvavidas*," we all repeated.

"Good," said Miss Holly. "The next word is 'toilet.' The Spanish word for 'toilet' is *el inodoro*."

"*El inodoro*," we all repeated.

This was getting weird. I figured Miss

Holly would teach us words we'd use every day, like "When do we eat?" or "Where is the skate park?" But she was teaching us weird words instead.

Neil the nude kid raised his hand. "Why do we need to learn *those* words?" he asked.

"Well," said Miss Holly, "what if you're at the beach and you need to tell somebody that the lifeguard's toupee fell in the toilet?"

Miss Holly is weird.

"Okay, that's enough vocabulary for now," Miss Holly said.

"Let's learn how they celebrate the holidays in a Spanish-speaking country like Mexico!"

Miss Holly told us that eleven days after Christmas in Mexico, kids put their shoes out on the balcony before they go to sleep. If they've been good, their shoes will be filled with treats when they wake up the next morning.

"Eww, that's disgusting!" I said. "I wouldn't eat those smelly treats!"

Miss Holly said that was silly. Then she told us that for nine days before

Christmas in Mexico, people act out the journey of Mary and Joseph going to Bethlehem. After a big feast, they play the piñata game.

"Repeat after me," said Miss Holly. "Piñata!"

"Piñata," we all repeated.

I knew what a piñata was because Ryan had one at his birthday party. It's this big, hollow, paper thing you hang from a tree, and kids take turns whacking it with a stick. When the piñata breaks open, candy falls out and everybody grabs it.

Piñatas are cool because you get to do two very cool things—eat candy and whack something with a stick.

Miss Holly went to the closet, and guess what she took out?

I'm not going to tell you.

Okay, okay, I'll tell you.

A piñata! It was in the shape of a star. We were going to play the piñata game! All right!

Miss Holly climbed up on her desk and tied the piñata to a bar on the ceiling.

"Can I go first?" we all yelled.

Miss Holly said we'd go in ABC order, which meant that Andrea (AN) got to go first. I lined up behind her because my real name, Arlo, begins with AR.

Miss Holly told us that in Mexico the kids are blindfolded when they play the piñata game. She tied a blindfold over Andrea's eyes and put a stick in her hand.

"You can do it, Andrea!" the girls yelled.

"I bet she misses the whole thing," I told Ryan.

Well, Andrea was totally pathetic. She hardly *ever* hit the piñata. Even when she did, she only tapped it a little and it just spun around. All the boys were cracking up.

Finally it was my turn. Miss Holly tied the blindfold over my eyes and put the stick in my hand.

"Kill it, A.J.!" the boys yelled.

No way was I going to let anybody laugh at *me*. I was going to whack that piñata so hard, candy would fly all over the room. I reached back and swung the stick as hard as I could.

But I must have missed.

"Owwww!" somebody screamed.

I took off the blindfold. Emily was lying on the floor with her hands over her head.

"A.J. hit me!" she yelled.

"It was an accident!" I said. I must admit I've always *wanted* to hit Emily with a stick, but I would never do it on purpose. It wasn't *my* fault that she got so close.

Miss Holly gasped. "Go to Mrs. Cooney's office," she told Emily. Mrs. Cooney is the school nurse.

Emily went running out of the room, shrieking like an elephant fell on her. What a crybaby! She wasn't even bleeding or anything.

I thought Miss Holly was going to let

me have another turn, but she said the piñata game was too dangerous to play in school. Bummer in the summer!

It wasn't fair. We didn't even get any candy.

Santa Klutz Is Coming to Town

"Line up in ABC order," said our teacher, Miss Daisy, after we finished pledging the allegiance the next morning. "We're having an assembly!"

"Yay!" said the girls.

"Boo!" said the boys.

Assemblies are when the whole school

goes to the all-purpose room and we have to listen to somebody talk for a million hundred hours. The last time we had an assembly, some children's book author told us about his books. What a bore! The reading specialist, Mr. Macky, is always trying to get us to read.

I hate reading.

But this assembly looked like it was going to be different. The all-purpose room was decorated with big candy canes, snowmen, and fake snow. "Jingle Bells" was playing on the loudspeaker.

After we sat down, the most amazing thing in the history of the world happened. Something started coming down from the ceiling above the stage!

At first we couldn't tell what it was. Then we saw it was a sleigh! As it got lower, we could see Santa Claus sitting in the sleigh. Some kids were pulling long ropes that lowered the sleigh down until it reached the stage.

"Ho ho ho!"

"It's Santa Claus!" everybody shouted.

"I'm not Santa Claus," the guy said. He took off his Santa hat so we could see his shiny bald head. "I'm Santa KLUTZ!"

It was Mr. Klutz, the principal! Everyone started hooting and hollering. Miss Daisy shushed us. Mr. Klutz waited until everybody was quiet. He picked up a microphone so we could hear him better.

"I always gets santamental around the holidays," Mr. Klutz said. "Get it? *Santa* mental?"

"Hahahahahahahahahaha!"

We all laughed even though Mr. Klutz didn't say anything funny. When the principal makes a joke, you should always laugh. That's the first rule of being a kid. If you don't laugh at the principal's jokes, he'll get mad and lock you in the dungeon down in the basement.

"But seriously," Mr. Klutz said, "what do you get when you cross a snowman with a vampire?"

"What?" we all yelled.

"Frostbite!" he said. "Get it? Frost? Bite?"

"Hahahahahahahaha!"

Mr. Klutz is always cracking jokes. He thinks he is a real comedian. But his jokes are terrible. It should be against the law for principals to tell jokes.

"Do you know why Santa's little helper was depressed?" Mr. Klutz asked.

"Why?" we all yelled.

"Because he had low elf-esteem. Get it? Elf? Esteem?"

"Hahahahahaha!"

Maybe if we stopped laughing at his jokes, Mr. Klutz would stop telling them.

"What do you call people who are afraid of Santa?" Mr. Klutz asked.

"What?" we all yelled.

"Claustrophobic!" he said. "Get it? Claus? Trophobic?"

"Hahahaha!"

It was horrible. It was like watching one of those movies that never ends. I looked over at Ryan and Michael. They rolled their eyes.

"What do snowmen eat for breakfast?" Mr. Klutz asked.

"What?" we all yelled.

"Snowflakes!" he said. "Get it? Snow? Flakes?"

"Haha!"

Finally Mr. Klutz ran out of jokes. What a relief! He told us he was dressed up like Santa because he had big news. This year Ella Mentry School would be putting on its first ever holiday pageant. That's a show all about the holidays.

"Our art teacher, Ms. Hannah, will help paint the scenery. Our music teacher, Mr. Loring, will help with the songs. Our librarian, Mrs. Roopy, will help with the research. And the director of the pageant," Mr. Klutz announced, "will be our own . . . Miss Holly!"

Everybody clapped, and Miss Holly danced up onto the stage with her guitar. She played "Winter Wonderland," and we all joined in.

"I'm so excited!" Miss Holly said. "We're going to sing songs, perform skits, and have lots of fun. It's going to be the best holiday pageant ever!"

It sounded horrible.

Secret Santa

After the assembly we walked a million hundred miles back to our class. Andrea was all excited about the holiday pageant. She loves to be in plays because she's a big show-off.

"Last year I was in *The Nutcracker*," she bragged.

"They made a play about nuts?" I asked. "No wonder *you* were in it."

Andrea got all mad. "Why do you have to be so mean, Arlo?"

"Why do you have to be so annoying?" I asked.

"Enough chitchatting," Miss Daisy said when we were all sitting in our seats. "I have some important news. This year we're going to have a Secret Santa in our class."

Secret Santa? Who's that? None of us had ever heard of Secret Santa. But Santa is cool, and anything that involves secrets is cool. So Secret Santa must be cool.

Miss Daisy told us that she wrote everyone's name on slips of paper and put them all into a fishbowl. Each of us would take a slip of paper out of the fishbowl, and then we'd have to get a present for that kid. But we couldn't tell the kid we were getting them a present. That's what made it a *secret*. Miss Daisy said we would exchange our Secret Santa presents in a few weeks, just before the big holiday pageant. If anyone forgot to bring in a present, they wouldn't be allowed to *get* a present either.

Everybody was all excited. We lined up to pick slips of paper out of the fishbowl. I hoped I wouldn't pick some lame girl like Andrea or Emily. I'd rather get a present for Ryan or Michael or one of the other boys.

We lined up in ZYX order, which is the opposite of ABC order. Everybody picked a slip of paper out of the fishbowl and giggled a little when they saw the name on it. Finally it was my turn. There were only a couple of slips of paper left.

"No peeking, A.J.," Miss Daisy told me

as I reached my hand into the fishbowl.

I picked out a slip of paper.

I looked at the paper.

The paper said . . .

I'm not going to tell you.

Okay, okay, I'll tell you.

The paper said, "Emily."

Noooooooooooooooooooooooo!

Not Emily! What could I possibly get for Emily? She is a real girly-girl. I will have to go to some girly-girl store and buy some girly-girl present like smelly perfume. It will be horrible.

Secret Santa is stupid.

Learning How to Speak Spanish

A few days later, we were in the language lab and Miss Holly was telling us all about Spain. It's a country in Europe, and it's the whole way across the Atlantic Ocean.

Miss Holly played her guitar, sang, tap-danced, and told us all kinds of useless information about Spain. Did you know that Spain is twice the size of Oregon? I didn't know that.

Do you care?

Me neither.

"In Spain," Miss Holly told us, "boys and girls only have to go to school until they are sixteen years old."

"All right!" I said. "I'm moving to Spain!"

"Then you'll have to learn to speak Spanish, A.J.," said Miss Holly.

I told her I already know how to speak Spanish because I saw this movie called *Terminator II* where Arnold Schwarzenegger kills a bunch of guys, and before he leaves he says, "*Hasta la vista*, baby!" My mom told me that means "until we meet again." It was a

cool movie.

"That's good, A.J., but you'll have to learn a lot more than that," Miss Holly said. "Let's work on our Spanish vocabulary for the pageant."

"Yay!" said the girls.

"Boo!" said the boys.

"The first word we're going to learn

today is 'nose,'" said Miss Holly. "The Spanish word for 'nose' is *la nariz,*" said Miss Holly.

"*La nariz,*" we all repeated.

"Good," said Miss Holly. "The next word is 'think.' The Spanish word for 'think' is *pensar.*"

"*Pensar,*" we all repeated.

"Good," said Miss Holly. "The next word is 'Christmas tree.' The Spanish word for 'Christmas tree' is *el árbol de Navidad.*"

"*El árbol de Navidad,*" we all repeated.

"Good," said Miss Holly. "The next word is 'stuck.' The Spanish word for 'stuck' is *pegado.*"

"Pegado," we all repeated.

Miss Holly sure picks weird words.

Neil the nude kid raised his hand. "Why do we need to learn those words?" he asked.

"Well," Miss Holly said, "what if you're in Spain and you need to say, 'I think I have a Christmas tree stuck to my nose'?"

Miss Holly is weird.

The Opposite
of Hanukkah

During the first week in December, Miss
Daisy told us all about the holidays so
we'd be ready for the pageant. I already
knew the story of Christmas. But I didn't
know much about Hanukkah.

Now, I don't remember *everything* Miss
Daisy told us. But basically, Hanukkah
has something to do with a war. I know

all about war. I have some plastic army guys down in my basement, and me and Michael and Ryan line them up and shoot them with rubber bands.

Anyway, a million hundred years ago, the Jewish people were fighting a war. They were way outnumbered by another army, but they kicked their butts anyway. So after the war was over, the Jewish people went back to their temple to hang out and play video games and stuff. It was dark out. They didn't have lightbulbs in those days, so they had to light oil lamps or they would bump into the walls when they walked into the kitchen to get more pizza.

The problem was that they could only find one jar of oil. That would last one night, but they wanted to hang out all week playing video games and eating pizza. I guess they sent somebody to the gas station to get more oil, but he never came back. So they put the one jar of oil they had into the lamp and lit it.

The cool thing is that the oil didn't just last one night. It didn't just last two nights. It didn't just last three nights. It lasted eight whole nights! It was a miracle!

"Wow!" we all said after Miss Daisy finished telling us the story of Hanukkah.

"I saw a miracle like that once," I said.

"Tell us about it, A.J.," said Miss Daisy.

"We were driving to my grandmother's house," I said. "Suddenly our car stopped right in the middle of the highway. My dad said he thought he had a full tank of gas, but it turned out the gas gauge was broken, and the tank was empty."

"That doesn't have anything to do with Hanukkah," Andrea said.

"Sure it does," I said. "The Jewish people thought they only had a little oil, but it turned out they had a lot. We thought we had a lot of gas, but we only had a little. It was the opposite of Hanukkah."

"You're a dumbhead," Andrea said.

"So is your face," I told her. Anytime somebody says something mean to you, all you have to do is say, "So is your face." That's the first rule of being a kid.

Miss Daisy told me and Andrea to

knock it off. She said that Hanukkah lasts for eight nights, and each night they light a candle in the menorah.

"They stick the candles in manure?" I asked. "That's disgusting!"

"Menor*ah*," Miss Daisy said. "It's like a candleholder."

"Oh," I said. "I knew that."

To celebrate Hanukkah, Jewish kids play this game with a four-sided top called a dreidel that spins around, and they eat potato pancakes called latkes, and they hunt for chocolate coins wrapped in gold foil. The kids get presents every night, too, of course. Hanukkah is cool.

Miss Daisy showed us how to spin a

dreidel and gave us each a piece of chocolate money. We had a bathroom break after that, and then she said it was time to work on our writing skills. We were learning to write friendly letters, so Miss Daisy asked us if we'd like to write letters to Santa Claus.

"Yeah!" everybody shouted.

She told us to write whatever we wanted. This is what I wrote:

Dear Santa,

Please bring me a dirt bike and a football and a skateboard and a remote-control car and that new video game where you get to kill zombies with machine guns. Also I need a new Striker Smith action figure because mine got run over by the school bus after Ryan threw it out the window. I'll take anything else you have lying around your workshop that is cool too. I love presents. But please don't bring me any boring stuff like clothes or books.

Miss Daisy looked at what I was writing and said I had to write something besides a list of stuff I want. So I added this:

Santa, I think you should lose some weight. On TV they keep saying that Americans weigh too much. Maybe if you worked more than one day a year, you would lose a few pounds. My mother lost twenty pounds on Weight Watchers. That might work for you.

Also, I don't think it was nice for the other reindeer to make fun of Rudolph, laughing and calling him names. That was mean. If I was Rudolph and they wouldn't let me play any

reindeer games, I would punch those
other reindeer in the nose.

    Sincerely,

    A.J.

    P.S. One more thing. Did you ever
hit your head on the North Pole?

Miss Daisy asked if anyone wanted to read their letter in front of the class. Andrea was the only one who raised her hand (of course), so she stood up and started reading.

Dear Santa,

    This year I don't want you to bring me anything. There are children all over the world who don't have any toys. So please take the toys you were going to give to me and give them to poor children instead. The world would be a better place if people had less toys and more peace and love.

Love,

Andrea

What a brownnoser! I know for a fact that Andrea only said that stuff so Miss Daisy would like her. Once I went to Andrea's house for her birthday party, and the place was *filled* with toys. She has every American Girl doll ever made. The only reason Andrea doesn't want Santa to bring her any more toys is because she has no place to put them.

After Andrea finished reading her

dumb letter, the most amazing thing in the history of the world happened. Miss Daisy started crying!

"That's the most beautiful letter I've ever heard, Andrea," said Miss Daisy.

Andrea smiled her Little-Miss-Perfect smile.

Why doesn't a sack filled with letters fall on her head?

Is Santa Claus Real?

That afternoon me and Michael and Ryan were in the vomitorium eating lunch. Andrea and Emily and their girly friends were at the next table, so they couldn't bother us.

It's noisy in the vomitorium! Everyone was hooting and hollering. The lunch lady, Ms. LaGrange, was wearing these antler earmuff thingies on her head to block out the sound.

Ms. LaGrange is strange.

I had a peanut butter and jelly sandwich. Michael had a tuna sandwich. Ryan had two slices of bread and some slices of ham. Instead of putting the ham between the bread slices, he put it on the *outside* of the bread. Then he started eating.

"Why did you put the ham on the *outside* of your sandwich?" I asked him.

"It's not a sandwich," Ryan replied. "It's a wichsand."

Ryan is weird.

"I'll bet Santa isn't going to read those

letters we wrote," Michael said as he bit into his sandwich.

"Santa doesn't even exist," Ryan said. "One time I saw this Santa guy on the street ringing a bell, and then on the next block, there was *another* Santa guy who looked just like him."

"Maybe the second one was a clone," I said. "My friend Billy who lives around the corner told me that they can take a cell from a sheep and clone it into a whole nother sheep."

"'Nother' isn't a word, A.J.," Michael said.

"Neither is your face," I told him.

"Look, it's just impossible for one guy to visit every single house in the world in one night," Ryan said. "Besides, our house doesn't even have a chimney. How would he get in?"

"If you don't have a chimney," Michael

said, "Santa comes in through the toilet bowl. Everybody has one of them."

"That's disgusting," I said. "And he couldn't fit through the toilet anyway."

"It's just impossible," Ryan insisted. "There's no way Santa could make toys for every kid in the world."

"He has Elvis to help him," I said.

Michael and Ryan looked at me.

"Not *Elvis*, dumbhead!" Michael yelled, slapping his forehead. "Elves! He has *elves* to help him!"

"I knew that."

At the table beside us, Andrea and her annoying friends were giggling. They must have been listening in on our private conversation.

"You better watch out, Arlo," Andrea said. "Santa has a list, and he's checking it twice."

"He knows if you've been bad or good," said Emily, "so be good for goodness' sake."

"Who asked you two?" I said.

"You're naughty," Andrea said. "But Emily and I are nice, so Santa is going to bring us good presents. He's probably going to bring you a lump of coal."

"That's okay," I said. "I'll give it away to some poor boys and girls who don't have any coal. Then we'll have more peace and love in the world."

Ryan and Michael cracked up. Nah-nah-nah boo-boo on Andrea! Why doesn't a giant lump of coal fall on her head?

8

Getting Ready for the Holiday Pageant

"*¡Buenos días!*" Miss Holly said a few days later. That means "good day" in Spanish. There were red and green balloons and streamers all over the hallways. Spanish Christmas music was playing. And Miss Holly had that basket of fruit on her head again.

Everybody was excited about our first rehearsal for the big holiday pageant. Everybody except the boys, that is.

When we got to the language lab, Miss Holly was up on a ladder taping little plants to the walls.

"What's that?" asked Neil the

nude kid.

"It's mistletoe!" said Miss Holly.

What a dumb name. Missiles blast into outer space. How can a missile have a toe? They should definitely get a new name for that plant.

Miss Holly told us that when two people are standing under mistletoe, they're supposed to kiss. Eww! Yuck! Disgusting! I'm not kissing anyone. And I'm sure not going to kiss anyone just because some *plant* told me to. Mistletoe is creepy. I'm not going anywhere near that stuff.

Miss Holly told us that besides Christmas and Hanukkah, there is another holiday people celebrate in December. It's an African American holiday called Kwanzaa. Ryan got all excited, because that's the holiday his family celebrates. Miss Holly asked him to tell us about it.

Ryan told us that Kwanzaa means "first fruits," and it celebrates the harvest of the crops. It starts the day after Christmas and lasts seven days. Each day you light a candle in this candleholder called a *kinara*. Then somebody will say *"Harambee,"* which means "Let's pull together" in Swahili.

It wasn't fair. Christmas only lasts one day. But Kwanzaa lasts seven days and Hanukkah lasts eight days. Man, I wish I was black or Jewish.

Ryan told us that on *kuumba*, the sixth day of Kwanzaa, they have a big feast called *karamu*. They eat fried okra, vegetable stew, squash, peanut soup, and sweet potato pie. Yuck! Ryan will eat anything. If I had to eat that stuff, I'd die.

But other than eating that yucky food, Kwanzaa sounded cool. Ryan taught us a Kwanzaa song called "Kuumba," and Miss Holly said it would be perfect for the holiday pageant. Then Miss Holly told us that we were going to have to wear costumes and memorize lines. The holiday pageant was sounding lamer and lamer. She also said she needed to pick kids for the speaking parts. All the girls got excited.

"Oooh, can I be the sugar plum fairy?" begged Andrea.

"Oooh, can I sing the dreidel song?" begged Emily.

"What about you boys?" asked Miss Holly. "Which speaking parts do you want?"

"We don't want any speaking parts," I announced.

"That's right," agreed Michael and Ryan.

"I won't force you to take a speaking part," Miss Holly said, "but you do have to be in the pageant. You three boys will be the stage crew."

"Stage crew?" I asked. "What's that?"

"That means you'll work the spotlight and move the scenery and props around," said Miss Holly.

Being on the stage crew sounded cool. I looked at Ryan and Michael to make sure they thought so too.

"No problemo," I said. That's Spanish for "no problem," in case you don't speak Spanish as well as me.

"But I'll still need you to wear costumes," Miss Holly said, "because we need elves. We must have elves! You can't have a holiday pageant without elves!"

"We don't want to be elves!" Michael said. "Elves are lame."

"Yeah, I'm not dressing up like

an elf," I said.

Miss Holly looked at us, and I could tell that she was getting mad because she put her hands on her hips. Whenever grown-ups put their hands on their hips, that means they're mad. Nobody knows why.

I was afraid Miss Holly might punish us by making us be sugar plum fairies. Then

we'd have to wear tights like my sister. That's when I got the greatest idea in the history of the world.

"Instead of dressing up like elves," I said, "can we dress up like *Elvis*?"

Miss Holly thought it over for a few seconds.

"Okay!" she finally agreed. "You three boys can be Elvis!"

All right! Maybe the holiday pageant wouldn't be so lame after all.

9

The Most Horrible Thing in the History of the World

A couple of days later, around two o'clock, we came into the all-purpose room for rehearsal. Miss Holly was wearing a Santa Claus hat and beard. She's weird.

"Habari gani?" she said.

"What the heck does that mean?" I asked.

"That means 'What's the news?' in Swahili," said Miss Holly. "You say it during Kwanzaa."

It was a week before the big holiday pageant, and we had to rehearse every day. There was a lot of work to do. We had Christmas, Hanukkah, and Kwanzaa songs to learn, lines to memorize, and entrances and exits to practice.

Me and Ryan and Michael had to learn

how to move the scenery and props around and work the spotlight, too. At the end of the pageant, it would be our job to lower Santa Claus (Mr. Klutz, of course) and his sleigh down from the ceiling with ropes. That was going to be cool.

Miss Holly said that because we were Elvises, we could sing "Hound Dog," even though it didn't have anything to do with the holidays. Mr. Loring, our music teacher, played piano for all the songs. Miss Holly played her guitar.

Emily got to sing a solo. She is a big crybaby, but she has a pretty good voice, and Miss Holly let her sing "The Dreidel

Song." Emily was practicing it when I came up with the most brilliant idea in the history of the world.

"Since she's singing a song about a dreidel," I said to Miss Holly, "maybe she should spin around too?"

"Great idea, A.J.!" said Miss Holly.

I'm in the gifted and talented program, and I'm constantly coming up with genius ideas. I should get the No Bell Prize for that one.

At the end of rehearsal, Miss Holly told us how proud she was. She said the holiday pageant was going to be great. Miss Holly was so pleased that she told us she was going to invite Dr. Carbles, the president of the Board of Education, to come and see the show. Wow! If the principal is the king of the school, the president of the Board of Education must be like the king of the whole world.

We rehearsed until three o'clock, when it was time for dismissal. Then we lined up outside the doorway in ABC order. That's when Andrea turned around and whispered in my ear, "Hey, Arlo. Look up!"

I looked up.

It was that mistletoe stuff! It was hanging from the doorway right over our heads! How did it get up there?

I remembered what Miss Holly told us about mistletoe. If two people are under it, they're supposed to kiss. Andrea was standing there with her lips all puckered up like she was trying to whistle. Eww! Yuck! Disgusting! What is her problem?

No way was I going to kiss Andrea. I didn't know what to say. I didn't know what to do. I had to think fast. I looked around to see if Ryan and Michael were watching.

"You have to kiss me, Arlo," Andrea whispered.

"I do not."

"Do too."

"No way."

"Yes way."

"Not in my lifetime."

"It's the rule, Arlo."

"Says who?"

"If you don't kiss me, you'll be in trouble, Arlo."

I'd rather be in trouble than kiss Andrea. I'd rather be run over by a herd of buffalo than kiss Andrea. I'd rather have an elevator fall on my head than kiss Andrea. I'd rather *die*—

I didn't get the chance to finish my thought, because at that very moment the most horrible thing in the history of the world happened.

Andrea kissed *me*!

Ugh! On the lips! I thought I was gonna throw up! Quickly I wiped my lips off. I

mean, I wiped off my lips. I mean, my lips stayed on, but I wiped them off. What I'm trying to say is I didn't want to be infected by Andrea's disgusting cooties. I just hoped nobody saw what happened.

"Oooooh!" Ryan said. "Andrea and A.J. just kissed. They must be in *love*!"

"When are you gonna get married?" asked Michael.

If those guys weren't my best friends, I would hate them.

My
Genius Idea

My life was over.

I ran home so fast I could have won a gold medal in the Olympics.

Now that Andrea had kissed me, going back to school was out of the question. I could never show my face there again. Ryan and Michael would never let me hear the end of it.

That's when I got a genius idea. I could get plastic surgery! My friend Billy who lives around the corner told me that some lady in France got a face transplant. The doctors just took somebody else's face and put it on her head. Cool! I could do that. I could get a new face and go back to school. Nobody would know it was me.

But getting a face transplant sounded disgusting. And my parents probably wouldn't get me one anyway. They wouldn't even get me a new Striker Smith action figure to replace the one Ryan threw out the bus window. No way were they going to get me a new face.

Now that Andrea had kissed me, I had no other choice. I had to move to Antarctica, where no human being would ever see me again. I would live with the penguins. Penguins are cool, and they wouldn't care that Andrea kissed me.

"Can you drive me to Antarctica?" I asked my mother after school. "I need to go live with the penguins for the rest of my life."

"Sure," she replied, "but first we have to go to the pet store."

Oh, I completely forgot! We were all out of fish food! My chore at home is to take care of our fish. Mom had told me first thing in the morning that after school we were going to the pet store to get fish food.

Mom says I have to do chores like feeding our fish because doing chores makes you a responsible person. That makes no sense at all. I'm *already* a responsible person. Any time something goes wrong, everybody says I'm responsible.

So we drove to the pet store. They have all kinds of animal stuff there. They even have Christmas presents for pets. People actually give gifts to their dogs!

Dog owners are weird.

You have to be real careful with fish. You have to feed them, clean their tank, and make sure the filter is working. I found the fish food and got in line with my mom to pay for it. There was a little sign in front of the cash register that said:

DID YOU FORGET ANYTHING?

Hmm, did I forget anything? That's when I suddenly remembered what I forgot. I forgot all about the Secret Santa present I was supposed to get for Emily! We had to bring them in tomorrow!

Oh, man! If I didn't bring in a Secret Santa present for Emily, I wouldn't get a present from *my* Secret Santa! And I *love* getting presents. I *had* to go back to school. If I went to Antarctica, I wouldn't get my Secret Santa present.

"Mom," I asked, "can you drive me to the mall after this?"

"I thought you wanted me to drive you to Antarctica."

"I changed my mind," I said. "I need to go to a smelly perfume store to get a Secret Santa present for Emily."

Mom was really mad. The stores are all crowded before Christmas, and the traffic is really bad. She said she didn't have time to take me to the smelly perfume store.

That's when I got another one of my genius ideas. I could get Emily a present right there at the pet store! They sell

goldfish for just ten cents. I could get
Emily a couple of goldfish. They would
make a way cooler present than smelly

perfume! And I wouldn't have to waste a lot of my money buying smelly perfume for that crybaby Emily, who I don't even like. The lady behind the counter even said she'd put the goldfish in a plastic bag filled with water and wrap it up in a box.

Haha! I'm a genius! That's why I'm in the gifted and talented program.

11

The Arrival of Secret Santa

I was nervous about going to school the next morning. I wanted to get my Secret Santa present, but I didn't want the guys to make fun of me for getting kissed by Andrea. I decided to stay away from her, no matter what.

I put my backpack in my cubby. Ryan

and Michael didn't even mention any-thing about me kissing Andrea. I guess they forgot about it.

After we pledged the allegiance, every-body got all excited because it was time to open our Secret Santa presents.

Ryan got a jigsaw puzzle from his Secret Santa. Michael got Legos from his Secret Santa. Neil the nude kid got a model plane from his Secret Santa. I kept waiting for my turn.

"Who is A.J.'s Secret Santa?" Miss Daisy finally asked.

"I am!"

It was Andrea! Oh man! If I had known that Andrea was my Secret Santa, I would have moved to Antarctica.

"Ooooooh!" Ryan said. "A.J. got a present from Andrea. She kissed him too. They must be in *love*!"

"When are you gonna get married?" asked Michael.

I told them to shut up. Andrea gave me the present. I tore off the wrapping paper and the dumb bow (which serves no purpose anyway). Then I opened the box. And do you know what was inside?

I'm not going to tell you.

Okay, okay, I'll tell you.

It was a hat.

A hat! Who gets a kid a hat? A hat isn't a present. A hat is clothes. It was horrible.

Not only that, but it looked just like the dumb hat Andrea wears all the time.

"I knitted it myself," Andrea said, "in my knitting class."

"How wonderful, Andrea!" said Miss Daisy. "A homemade present is so much nicer than something you buy in a store.

A.J., what do you say to Andrea?"

No way was I going to wear a hat that looked just like Andrea's dumb hat. I didn't know what to say. I didn't know what to do. I had to think fast.

"I hate hats," I said.

"You're mean!" Andrea said.

Miss Daisy made me apologize to Andrea, so I told her I was sorry she made me a dumb hat.

"Who is Emily's Secret Santa?" asked Miss Daisy.

"I am," I said.

I took out the present and gave it to Emily. I was so excited because my present was way cooler than all the others.

She opened it up.

"What is it?" everybody asked.

Emily pulled the plastic bag out of the box and started crying.

"It's a dead fish!" she sobbed. "I can't believe you got me a dead fish for Christmas, A.J.!"

"It wasn't dead when I *got* it!" I said. "And there were two of them. Where's the other one?"

"They must have eaten each other," said Ryan. "Stuff like that happens all the time with fish, you know."

"Man, that's twenty cents I wasted," I said.

"This is going to be a *terrible* Christmas," Emily cried as she went running out of the room, "and A.J. is responsible!"

See? I told you I was responsible.

The Big
Holiday Pageant

Finally the day of the big holiday pageant arrived. Everybody came to school in their costumes. Miss Holly wore a Santa suit. Me and Ryan and Michael wore black jackets and had our hair greased up so we looked like Elvis. It was cool.

We peeked through the curtains from

backstage. The all-purpose room was packed with parents. A bunch of them were setting up video cameras to record the show.

"Guess what?" Miss Holly said. "Dr. Carbles, the president of the Board of Education, is here! He's sitting in the front row! Let's put on a great show for him."

The stage was decorated with big candy canes, snowmen, fake snow, and a

giant reindeer. It looked great. Miss Holly nodded to me and Ryan and Michael. We pulled a long rope to open the curtain.

The show started out with one of the fifth-grade classes telling the story of Christmas. After that me and Michael and Ryan sang "Hound Dog." Everybody went crazy! After that one of the fourth-grade classes told the story of Kwanzaa. After that we sang "Winter Wonderland." After that one of the third-grade classes told the story of Hanukkah. After that Emily sang "The Dreidel Song."

"Dreidel, dreidel, dreidel, I made it out of clay. . . ."

Me and Michael and Ryan were taking

turns working the spotlight, and it was my turn. I shone the light on Emily while she sang and spun around.

"The light is too high, A.J.," Ryan said. "You're shining it in her eyes."

"I am not," I said.

"Are too," he said.

We went back and forth like that for a while, but we didn't get the chance to finish the argument, because the most amazing thing in the history of the world happened.

While Emily was singing and spinning around, she must have slipped on some fake snow or something because she fell off the stage! You should have been

there! When Emily was falling, she tried to grab hold of the giant reindeer. But it wasn't nailed down or anything, and the two of them fell into the front row and landed on Dr. Carbles, the president of the Board of

Education! It was a real Kodak moment.

People were screaming. Mrs. Cooney, the nurse, ran over to make sure Emily was okay. The reindeer's head fell off, and some of the kindergarten kids started crying. It was hilarious. And we got to see it live and in person.

Miss Holly ran onto the stage and told the audience there would be a short intermission. Backstage, all the girls were upset. All the boys were laughing our heads off.

"This is the worst holiday pageant ever!" said Andrea. "And Arlo is responsible."

"Me?" I asked. "What did I do?"

"It was your idea for Emily to spin around," she said, "and you shined the spotlight in her eyes. That's why she fell off the stage. Now everything is a big mess!"

"So is your face," I told her.

Miss Holly said we should both calm down. She said the show was still great, and that we should get ready for the big finale. All the kids in the school were going to gather on the stage and sing "Jingle Bells" while Santa's Elvises (that's us) lowered Mr. Klutz and his sleigh full of presents down from the ceiling.

Everybody got into position. Mr. Klutz climbed into the sleigh in his Santa costume. Ryan pulled open the curtains. Me and Michael grabbed the ropes to lower the sleigh down from the ceiling. The parents started clapping.

"'Jingle Bells, jingle bells, jingle all the way . . .'"

Me and Michael pulled on the ropes. The only problem was, my rope was stuck.

"My rope is stuck!" I yelled over to Michael.

But he couldn't hear me over the music. He kept pulling his rope.

"'Oh what fun it is to ride in a one-horse

open sleigh—hey!'"

I looked up at the sleigh. The front of it was coming down, but the back part was stuck.

The sleigh was tilting forward. Mr. Klutz was going to fall!

I tried to get my rope loose, but it was still stuck. Michael kept lowering the front end of the sleigh. Mr. Klutz reached up and grabbed one of the poles on the ceiling.

"'Jingle Bells, jingle bells, jingle all the—'"

The kids didn't get the chance to finish their song because all the presents that were in the sleigh tumbled out and fell on their heads. Some of the parents started screaming. Mr. Klutz was hanging

from the pole near the ceiling. I guess it was the North Pole. Hahaha!

"Help! Help!" he yelled.

Mr. Klutz's Santa hat and fake beard fell off. The beard

landed on some first grader's head. She freaked out and threw it into the audience. It landed on some lady. She screamed and threw it off her like it was a dead animal. It landed on some other lady, and she screamed too. The parents were throwing the beard around the all-purpose room. The custodian, Miss Lazar, ran to get a ladder so she could rescue Mr. Klutz.

"Those Elvises ruined the show!" some kid shouted.

I looked at Ryan. Ryan looked at Michael. Michael looked at me. We didn't have to say anything. The three of us made a run for the exit in the back of

the all-purpose room.

"It's Arlo's fault," Andrea hollered. "He's responsible!"

"The Elvises have left the building," Michael yelled as we ran out the door.

"*Hasta la vista,* baby!" I yelled.

We ran out of there as fast as we could.

I don't know if we'll ever go back.

Well, that's what happened at our big holiday pageant. Maybe me and Ryan and Michael will have to go live in Antarctica for the rest of our lives. Maybe Miss Holly will go live in Spain. Maybe the video of Emily falling off the stage will be on *America's Funniest Home Videos*. Maybe me and Ryan and Michael will be allowed to come back to school. Maybe we'll have a better holiday pageant next year. Maybe Miss Lazar will be able to get Mr. Klutz down from the North Pole.

But it won't be easy!

Check out the My Weird School series!

#1: Miss Daisy Is Crazy!
Pb 0-06-050700-4
The first book in the hilarious series stars A.J., a second grader who hates school—and can't believe his teacher hates it too!

#2: Mr. Klutz Is Nuts!
Pb 0-06-050702-0
A.J. can't believe his crazy principal wants to climb to the top of the flagpole!

#3: Mrs. Roopy Is Loopy!
Pb 0-06-050704-7
The new librarian at A.J.'s weird school thinks she's George Washington one day and Little Bo Peep the next!

#4: Ms. Hannah Is Bananas!
Pb 0-06-050706-3
Ms. Hannah, the art teacher, wears clothes made from pot holders and collects trash. Worse than that, she's trying to make A.J. be partners with yucky Andrea!

#5: Miss Small Is off the Wall!
Pb 0-06-074518-5
Miss Small, the gym teacher, is teaching A.J.'s class to juggle scarves, balance feathers, and do everything *but* play sports!

#6: Mr. Hynde Is Out of His Mind!
Pb 0-06-074520-7
The music teacher, Mr. Hynde, raps, break-dances, and plays bongo drums on the principal's bald head! But does he have what it takes to be a real rock-and-roll star?

#7: Mrs. Cooney Is Loony!
Pb 0-06-074522-3
Mrs. Cooney, the school nurse, is everybody's favorite—but is she hiding a secret identity?

#8: Ms. LaGrange Is Strange!
Pb 0-06-082223-6
The new lunch lady, Ms. LaGrange, talks funny—
and why is she writing secret messages in the
mashed potatoes?

#9: Miss Lazar Is Bizarre!
Pb 0-06-082225-2
What kind of grown-up *likes* cleaning throw-up?
Miss Lazar is the weirdest custodian in the his-
tory of the world!

#10: Mr. Docker Is off His Rocker!
Pb 0-06-082227-9
Mr. Docker, the science teacher, alarms and
amuses A.J.'s class with his wacky experiments
and nutty inventions.

#11: Mrs. Kormel Is Not Normal!
Pb 0-06-082229-5
A.J.'s school bus gets a flat tire, then becomes
hopelessly lost at the hands of Mrs. Kormel, the
wacky bus driver.

#12: Ms. Todd Is Odd!
Pb 0-06-082231-7
Ms. Todd is subbing, and A.J. and his friends are
sure she kidnapped Miss Daisy so she could take
over her job. Ms. Todd is the weirdest substitute
teacher in the history of the world.

#13: Mrs. Patty Is Batty!
Pb 0-06-085380-8
In this special Halloween installment, a little bit
of spookiness and a lot of humor add up to the
best trick-or-treating adventure ever!

Also look for
#15: Mr. Macky Is Wacky!

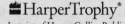
HarperTrophy®
An Imprint of HarperCollinsPublishers

www.dangutman.com

Dr. Carbles Is Losing His Marbles!

Dan Gutman

Pictures by
Jim Paillot

HarperTrophy®
An Imprint of HarperCollins Publishers

Dr. Carbles Is Losing His Marbles!
Text copyright © 2007 by Dan Gutman
Illustrations copyright © 2007 by Jim Paillot
All rights reserved. Printed in the United States of America.
No part of this book may be used or reproduced in any manner whatsoever without
written permission except in the case of brief quotations embodied in critical articles
and reviews. For information address HarperCollins Children's Books, a division of
HarperCollins Publishers, 195 Broadway, New York, NY 10007.
www.harpercollinschildrens.com

Library of Congress Cataloging-in-Publication Data
Gutman, Dan.
    Dr. Carbles is losing his marbles! / Dan Gutman ; pictures by Jim Paillot.— 1st Harper
Trophy ed.
        p. cm. — (My weird school ; #19)
    Summary: Tired of following the strict rules of their grumpy replacement principal as
Thanksgiving approaches, second-grader A.J. and his classmates try to find a way to
bring back eccentric but lovable Principal Klutz, who was fired for bringing a wild
turkey to school.
    ISBN 978-0-06-123477-4 (pbk. bdg.) – ISBN 978-0-06-123478-1 (lib. bdg.)
    [1. Schools–Fiction. 2. School principals–Fiction. 3. Humorous stories.] I. Paillot, Jim,
ill. II. Title.
PZ7.G9846Dr 2007   2007009129
[Fic]—dc22   CIP
                                                                      AC

Typography by Joel Tippie
21 BRR 32
❖
First Harper Trophy edition, 2007

To Emma

Contents

Squanto and Pocahontas

My name is A.J. and I hate school.

Do you know what the only good part of school is? The *end* of it, at three o'clock, when we get to go home!

But at the end of school this one day in November, we weren't allowed to go home at three. The school secretary, Mrs. Patty, made an announcement that everybody had to go to the all-purpose room. (That's a room we use for all purposes, so it has the perfect name.)

Bummer in the summer!

So we were sitting there, bored out of our minds, when suddenly two American Indians came running down the aisle! They were wearing feathers and head-dresses. They jumped onto the stage, whooping and hollering.

But they couldn't fool us. We knew exactly who they were.

"It's Mrs. Roopy!" yelled my friend Michael, who never ties his shoes. Mrs. Roopy is our librarian.

"And Mr. Klutz!" yelled my friend Ryan, who will eat anything, even stuff that isn't food. Mr. Klutz is our principal, and he has no hair.

"Klutz?" said Mr. Klutz. "Never heard of him. I am Squanto, a Patuxet Indian who helped the Pilgrims survive their first years in America."

"And I am Pocahontas," said Mrs. Roopy. "I helped the English colonists when they arrived in Virginia in 1607."

Mrs. Roopy always dresses up like somebody else. She never admits she's the librarian.

Mrs. Roopy is loopy.

"Thanksgiving is coming up," said Mr.

Klutz. "To celebrate, we want to introduce you to a friend of ours."

They went behind the curtain, and you'll never believe in a million hundred years who they brought out onstage with them.

I'm not going to tell you.

Okay, okay, I'll tell you. But you have to read the next chapter. So nah-nah-nah boo-boo on you.

Turkeys Are Weird

It was a turkey! They brought a turkey right out onstage!

Now, I've seen plenty of dead turkeys in sandwiches, but I've never seen a live one before. This turkey was dressed like a Pilgrim, with a little bonnet and dress. It was hilarious. All the kids went nuts.

"Gobble, gobble," said the turkey.

"Where do you think Mr. Klutz got a turkey?" asked Neil Crouch, who we call Neil the nude kid even though he wears clothes.

"Maybe he rented it," said Michael. "You can rent anything. There's

probably a place called Rent-a-Turkey."

"For my birthday party, my parents rented a lady dressed like a clown," said Ryan. "If you can rent a lady dressed like a clown, then you can probably rent a turkey dressed like a lady."

"For *my* birthday party, my parents rented a pony," said this annoying girl with curly brown hair named Andrea Young. "We all got pony rides."

Why can't a pony fall on her head?

Mr. Klutz had his arms wrapped around the turkey so she couldn't escape. She didn't look very happy.

"This is our friend Gobbles," said Mrs. Roopy. "She's going to help us get into the spirit of Thanksgiving."

Everybody yelled "HELLO" to Gobbles.

"Gobble, gobble," said Gobbles, flapping her wings. Mr. Klutz was having a hard time holding on to her.

"Isn't Gobbles cute?" asked Andrea.

"No," I said.

What is her problem? Turkeys aren't *cute*. Penguins are cute. Turkeys are ugly. If they were cute, we wouldn't eat them. You don't see anybody eating penguins, do you? Besides, if Andrea thinks something is cute, then I don't.

"Gobble, gobble," said Gobbles again. She was really flapping her wings hard now.

Turkeys are weird. They can't fly. What's

the point of being a bird if you can't fly? That would be like being a fish that can't swim. Gobbles was probably upset because Thanksgiving was coming. If I was a turkey, I would hate Thanksgiving, too.

"I'll make a deal with you," said Mr. Klutz, who is always making deals with us. "If each class creates a beautiful Thanksgiving display, I will get married to Gobbles."

Wow! It would be cool to see Mr. Klutz marry a turkey. This was going to be even better than the time he kissed a pig on the lips.

Everybody was going crazy, cheering and stamping their feet. Gobbles didn't seem to like all that noise. She started

gobbling really loud. Then she freaked

out and broke away from Mr. Klutz!

Gobbles went running off the stage! She

jumped into the front row, where

the first graders sit! The

first graders freaked out,

shrieking and crying and running away!
Then *everybody* started freaking out!

"Run for your lives!" shouted Neil the
nude kid. "There's a wild turkey on the
loose!"

All the kids were screaming and running and crashing into each other. You
should have been there!

And you'll never believe who
came into the all-purpose room at
that very moment.

It was Dr. Carbles, the president of the Board of Education!

I always thought Mr. Klutz was important, like he was the king of the school. But if Mr. Klutz is like the king of the school, then Dr. Carbles is like the king of the *world.* He probably sits on a throne and has servants fan him with big feathers. I saw that in a movie once.

"KLUTZ!" he hollered. "What's the meaning of this? Why is it that every time I come to this school, you're in some weird costume and the students are running around like lunatics?"

"It's just a little discipline problem, sir," Mr. Klutz said as he chased Gobbles around. "I'm going to put Gobbles in

detention."

"Don't you have any sense, Klutz?" shouted Dr. Carbles. "We have enough discipline problems with the children. Why would you bring a turkey to school?"

"To marry it," somebody said.

That's when Gobbles went berserk. She crashed into Dr. Carbles and knocked him down!

"That's it, Klutz!" Dr. Carbles yelled. "You're FIRED!"

Meet the New Boss

What?! Mr. Klutz was *fired*? It couldn't be true! We were all shocked.

I thought it was one of those times when something really horrible happens and then it turns out just to be a dream. I saw that in a movie once.

But the next morning while we were putting our backpacks away, everybody was talking about what happened.

"Dr. Carbles can't fire Mr. Klutz!" said Michael.

"Well, he *did*," said Ryan.

"But Mr. Klutz is the best principal in the world!" said Neil the nude kid.

Neil was right. Everybody loved Mr. Klutz. I was sad. Some kids were crying. Teachers were hugging each other in the hallway and dabbing their eyes with tissues. It was like Mr. Klutz had died.

After we pledged the allegiance, our teacher, Miss Daisy, said we should remember the good times we had with Mr. Klutz.

"Remember when he got his foot caught at the top of the flagpole and was hanging upside down?" said Ryan.

"Remember when he dressed like Santa in the holiday pageant, and he was hanging upside down from his sleigh?" said Michael.

"Once I got called to his office, and he was hanging upside down

from the ceiling," I told everybody.

"Mr. Klutz sure hangs upside down a lot," said Emily, who is a big crybaby.

It was hard to concentrate on reading and math that morning. We were all thinking about the good old days with Mr. Klutz. When it was time to go to the vomitorium for lunch, we were still talking about him.

"They'll have to get us a new principal," said Andrea, who was sitting with her annoying girl friends at the next table.

"Who do you think it will be?" asked Ryan.

"I hope he's nice," said Emily, who always hopes everybody will be nice.

"How do you know it will be a *he*?" said

Andrea. "Maybe the principal will be a lady."

"Maybe one of the teachers will become principal," Michael said. "Like Mr. Docker or Ms. Hannah."

"Being principal is an important job," said Neil the nude kid. "There's lots to do, like yell at kids and boss around teachers."

"And dress up in weird costumes and marry turkeys," I added.

"It will be hard to find someone who can fill Mr. Klutz's shoes," said Andrea.

"Who cares about filling his shoes?" I said. "We just need a new principal. What would they fill his shoes with anyway?"

"It's just an expression, dumbhead,"

Andrea said.

"So is your face," I told her.

We didn't have to wait long to find out who the new principal would be. At the end of the day, we had to go to the all-purpose room again. Once everybody was seated, a lady got up onstage. She told us her name was Mrs. Haney and she was the superintendent of all the schools in the county.

Wow! And we thought Dr. Carbles was important. If Dr. Carbles is like the king of the world, then Mrs. Haney is like the queen of the *universe*.

"I bet she can fly and see through walls," I whispered to Michael. "That's

why she's Super Intendent."

Mrs. Haney said she knew we were sad about Mr. Klutz and told us not to worry. Nothing would change now that he was gone.

"I'd like to introduce you to your *new* principal," she announced.

And you'll never believe in a million

hundred years who walked out on the stage.

I'm not going to tell you.

Okay, okay, I'll tell you. And you don't even have to read the next chapter.

It was Dr. Carbles!

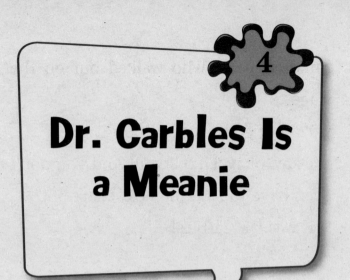

Dr. Carbles Is a Meanie

DR. CARBLES?!!?!?!?!?!?!?!?!?!?!?!?!?!?!?!?!?!?!

I always thought you had to go to principal school to be a principal. But I guess any dumbhead can be a principal.

Dr. Carbles wasn't wearing his usual jacket and tie. He was wearing an army uniform, with black boots and a whistle around his neck. In one hand he was holding a bullhorn. In the other he had a whip.

He didn't say anything at first. He just walked down the aisle, looking us over. Nobody made a move. Nobody made a sound. It was so quiet, you could hear a pin drop.*

We were all afraid of Dr. Carbles. He had a scowl on his face. Even Miss Daisy looked scared.

Finally Dr. Carbles put the bullhorn to his mouth.

---

*I mean one of those skinny little pins you use to sew stuff, not a bowling pin. Bowling pins actually make a *lot* of noise when they drop. But you could have heard one of those drop, too, it was so quiet.

"ATTEN—TION!" Dr. Carbles hollered, and we all straightened up in our seats. "This school is pathetic! You are unruly! You are undisciplined! You are totally disrespectful! I won't stand for it!"

He was really mad!

"You don't go to school to have *fun!*" he shouted. "You go to school to *learn*, so you can get into college and have a productive life."

"But I'm only in first grade!" said one of the first graders. Then she started to cry.

"Silence!" shouted Dr. Carbles. He cracked his whip, and everybody jumped. "There are going to be some changes around here. Mr. Klutz was too easy on you. There will be no more turkeys and silly costumes and contests. From now on we will focus on the four Rs: reading, writing, arithmetic, and rules.** We're going to

---

**That didn't make any sense at all, because only two of those words started with R.

25

turn you students into lean, mean learning machines. And if you don't like the way I do things, well, maybe you'd like to spend a little time in the dungeon on the third floor. Do I make myself clear?"

"Yes, Dr. Carbles," everybody mumbled.

"Children behave better when they're wearing uniforms," Dr. Carbles told us. "So from now on, you will wear the official uniform of Ella Mentry School."

The PTA moms went up and down the rows, passing out a bag to each of us.

"That's all for now," Dr. Carbles said. "Any questions?"

"Can I go to the bathroom?" somebody asked.

"No!" Dr. Carbles yelled. "Weak bladders lead to weak minds. Do you think George Washington went to the bathroom when he was crossing the Delaware?"

"They had bathrooms on the Delaware?" asked Ryan.

"Will we still have recess?" somebody else asked.

"No!" Dr. Carbles yelled. "Recess is for wimps."

"Will we still be allowed to play in the playground after school?" Michael asked.

"NO!" Dr. Carbles yelled. "You're going to MARCH in the playground after school."

Sure enough, when the three-o'clock

bell rang, Dr. Carbles led us out onto the playground. We had to form a line, with the fifth graders at the front and the kindergarten trolls at the back.

"Left! Right! Left! Right!" Dr. Carbles yelled as we marched. "Stop lagging

behind, kindergarteners!"

Dr. Carbles had us march around the playground a million hundred times. I thought I was gonna die.

Being Frank

The next morning everybody was wearing the official school uniform. The boys had on light blue shirts, blue pants, and blue ties. The girls had on blue skirts with stripes on them.

I looked like a dork. But *everybody* looked like a dork, so I didn't feel so bad.

We were putting our backpacks away when Mrs. Patty's voice came over the loudspeaker.

"A.J., please report to Dr. Carbles's office."

"Ooooooooooooooh!" everybody went.

"A.J. is absent today," I lied.

"Get down here, A.J.," said Mrs. Patty.

"Ooooooooooooooh!"

"You're in trouble, Arlo," said Andrea.

"Dr. Carbles is going to send you to jail."

What did I do? I mean, I know I did a lot of bad stuff. But not recently. It had been *weeks* since I wrote in the boys' bathroom that Andrea was a poopy head. Maybe Dr. Carbles was going to torture me in the dungeon on the third floor. Who knew what he might do to me?

I decided to take my time getting to Dr. Carbles's office. So I started counting the tiles in the hallway.

Did you know that there are 4,324 tiles between Miss Daisy's class and Dr. Carbles's office? I didn't.

As I was walking down the hall, a thought popped into my head. Maybe Dr.

Carbles was going to give me a candy bar! One time I got in trouble and had to go to Mr. Klutz's office. I thought he was going to punish me, but he gave me a candy bar instead. It was the greatest day of my life.

Finally I opened the door to Dr. Carbles's office. It looked a lot different from when Mr. Klutz was principal. The cool snowboarding poster was gone. The Foosball table and the punching bag were gone. Do you know what Dr. Carbles had all over his office instead?

Fish!

There was a fish tank on the windowsill. There was a fishing pole in the

corner. Dr. Carbles even had a picture of himself with a giant fish he'd caught. There was even a real fish that was mounted on the wall.

People who like fish that much are weird.

"What took you so long?" Dr. Carbles asked.

I didn't know what to say. I didn't know what to do. I had to think fast.

"I broke my leg," I lied.

"Shake it off!" Dr. Carbles ordered. "Do you think a broken leg would have stopped George Washington when he was crossing the Delaware?"

"I guess not," I said.

"A.J.," he said more softly, "do you know why I called you in here?"

"Because I wrote in the boys' bathroom that Andrea was a poopy head?"

"What?" yelled Dr. Carbles. "You wrote in the boys' bathroom that Andrea was a poopy head?"

"Uh, no," I said quickly. "What gave you that idea?" It was weird just hearing a principal say "poopy head."

"A.J., can I be Frank?" Dr. Carbles asked.

"I don't care what you call yourself," I told him.

"I asked you to come here because I need to talk with an average student," he said. "Do you know why I fired Mr. Klutz?"

"Because he wanted to marry a turkey?" I guessed.

"No, I fired Mr. Klutz because he's incompetent."

"He wears diapers?" I asked.

"Not incontinent!" Dr. Carbles yelled. "Incompetent! It means he didn't do a good job."

"But we all love Mr. Klutz," I said.

"A.J., I'm going to be Frank," said Dr. Carbles.

"Okay, Frank. I'll be A.J."

"I've never been a principal before," he admitted. "This is all new to me. I need to know what it is about Mr. Klutz that you kids love so much."

"I guess it's because he's silly," I said. "Mr. Klutz is like a big kid."

"A.J., let me be Frank," said Dr. Carbles.

"I already said you could be Frank," I told him.

"It's just not in my nature to be silly," Dr. Carbles said. "When I see the shenanigans at your school, I'm disgusted."

I didn't know what "shenanigans" were, but I didn't tell him that. I bet Andrea knows. She read the whole encyclopedia so she could show off how smart she is. What's up with that?

"If you don't like our shenanigans, maybe we could get some new shenanigans," I suggested.

"A.J., let's be Frank," Dr. Carbles said.

I slapped my forehead.

"You mean *both* of us?" I asked. "Won't that be confusing?"

"Enough! I know what you're trying to do, young man. You're trying to mess with my mind. Well, it won't work. Get out of my office!"

"Okay, Frank," I said.

I got up to leave but stopped at the door.

"Can I have a candy bar, Frank?" I asked.

"No! And stop calling me Frank!"

Sheesh, what a sourpuss! *He's* the one who said to call him Frank.

If you ask me, Dr. Carbles needs to take a chill pill.

Dr. Carbles Is Watching You

When I got back to class, everybody was working on our Thanksgiving display. Miss Daisy said we should still make one even if Mr. Klutz wasn't our principal anymore.

We spent all morning learning about Thanksgiving. The first one was in 1621, and it went on for three days. That's a long meal! Back then the Pilgrims only had knives and spoons. They didn't have any forks. Maybe if they had forks, it wouldn't have taken them three days to eat dinner.

Did you know that at the first Thanksgiving the Pilgrims didn't just eat turkey? They also ate ducks, geese, and swans. Ugh, disgusting!

It was fun making the display, but nobody was happy. We all knew that in the afternoon there would be more marching, more yelling, and more rules.

When we got to the vomitorium for lunch, all the posters about exercising and the Food Pyramid were gone. There

were new posters that said NO TALKING!,

BEHAVE, OR ELSE!, and SHUT UP AND EAT!

There was even a video camera mounted

on the wall with a sign under it that said

DR. CARBLES IS WATCHING YOU. We had to

whisper, because none of us wanted to

get sent to Dr. Carbles's office.

"I heard Dr. Carbles is going to put up guard towers and barbed wire around the school so we can't escape," Ryan whispered.

"We may have to dig a tunnel to get out," I whispered to the guys. "I saw that in a movie once."

"I heard that he punishes kids by putting them into solitary confinement," whispered Michael.

"They're forced to play solitaire?" I whispered back.

"Solitary confinement isn't the same as solitaire, dumbhead," whispered Andrea, who was sitting at the next table.

"Is too," I whispered.

We whispered back and forth like that for a while until I had to whisper "So is your face" to Andrea. But I knew I was right, because my mom plays that game solitary confinement on her computer.

"I miss Mr. Klutz," whispered Emily.

"I'm worried about him," whispered Andrea. "My mother is a psychologist, and she said that people who lose their jobs can get depressed."

"We've got to do something!" Emily whispered.

"We should go over to his house and cheer him up," Michael whispered.

"How would we find out where he

lives?" whispered Neil the nude kid.

"My mother is vice president of the PTA," Andrea whispered. "She knows everything."

Suddenly Dr. Carbles burst into the vomitorium with his bullhorn.

"Knock it off!" he yelled. "It's time for the lunchtime march! Let's go!"

We all jumped up and got into line outside the door.

"Hop to it!" Dr. Carbles hollered. "Left! Right! March! Move it, kindergarteners! You're slow and weak! I want each of you to give me twenty push-ups!"

Dr. Carbles is losing his marbles!

The Truth About Dr. Carbles

Well, I had to admit that Andrea came through for us. Her mother got Mr. Klutz's address, and on Saturday we all piled into her van to go visit him.

The van was big enough to hold Andrea, Emily, me, Ryan, Michael, and Neil the nude kid. Andrea's mom needs a big van because she is always taking

Andrea and her annoying girly friends to dance lessons and cooking lessons and piano lessons and every other kind of lessons they have. If they gave lessons on how to clip your toenails, Andrea would take them so she could get better at it.

I was really surprised when we got to Mr. Klutz's address. I thought he would live in a castle, since he was king of the school. But it was just a regular old house. Ryan rang the doorbell, and a lady came out.

"May I help you?" she asked. "I'm Karla Klutz."

Wow! Mr. Klutz never told us he had a wife! I wonder if she knew her husband was going to marry a turkey.

"Is Mr. Klutz home?" Andrea's mom asked.

"Yes, please come inside."

She led us into the living room. And you'll never believe in a million hundred years what we saw in there.

It was a half-pipe!

Mr. Klutz had a giant half-pipe right in the middle of his living room! Not only that, but he was skateboarding on it! He

did a frontside 180 ollie and a handstand fingerflip and a coconut wheelie. He was really good!

"Wooooo-hooooooooooooo!" yelled Mr. Klutz. "Watch this!"

He tried to do an inverted nosegrab, but he messed up, and it turned into a spectacular faceplant.***

"Are you okay?" we all asked as we ran over to help him.

"Of course!" he said. "To what do I owe the pleasure of your company?" (That's grown-up talk for "What are you doing here?")

"We were afraid you'd be depressed,"

***That means he crashed, in case you don't speak Skateboard.

50

Andrea told him, "so we came to cheer you up."

"Me? Depressed?" said Mr. Klutz. "I've never been happier! I don't have to write reports anymore or deal with crazy teachers, pushy parents, or obnoxious kids. Finally, I have time to chase my dream."

"What's your dream?" Neil the nude kid asked.

"To become a championship skateboarder," Mr. Klutz said.

"Cool!" said all the boys.

"But you're a great principal!" said Andrea, who never misses the chance to brownnose a grown-up. "We need you back at school."

"Dr. Carbles is driving us crazy," Michael said.

"Yes, Milton can be a bit hard to deal with," said Mr. Klutz.

"Milton?!" I said. "He told me his name was Frank!"

"I don't know about that," said Mr. Klutz, "but do you know why he fired me?"

"Because you wear diapers?" I asked.

"No," Mr. Klutz said. "Milton and I grew up together. He was my rival when we were teenagers. We were the two best skaters on the local skateboarding team. Then one day we got into an argument and I called him Walrus Face. From then on, *everybody* called him Walrus Face. He's been out to get me ever since."

"That's an insult," I said, "to walruses!"

"Hold on," said Andrea. "Dr. Carbles has been out to get you all these years just because you gave him a silly nickname?"

"There's more to it than that," Mr. Klutz told us. "Milton was also jealous of me because he went bald at a very young age and I had a full head of hair."

"YOU HAD A FULL HEAD OF HAIR?!" we all said at the same time.

Mr. Klutz has *no* hair at all. I mean *none*.

"Did you think I was born this way?" Mr. Klutz asked.

Mrs. Klutz brought out a photo album

with pictures of Mr. Klutz as a teenager. He had hair down to his shoulders!

"That's sad that your hair stopped growing," said Emily. It looked like there

Me and milton

were tears in her eyes. What a crybaby!

"Oh, it didn't stop growing," Mr. Klutz told us. "It still grows. Only now it grows out of my ears and nose. I have to trim it every week."

Ew, disgusting! I thought I was gonna throw up.

"Wait a minute," Andrea said. "Dr. Carbles isn't bald."

"Yes he is," said Mr. Klutz. "He wears a toupee. Shhhh! Don't tell him I told you. If people found out he's bald, it would drive him crazy."

Andrea's mother said it was time for us to go. Mr. Klutz thanked us for coming.

Just before we pulled out of the driveway,

Mrs. Klutz came running over to the van.

"He's driving me crazy at home!" she said. "You've *got* to get him back to school!"

Far-out, Man!

The next day it was more of the same at school. No talking. No smiling. No laughing. No fun.

Since it was raining at three o'clock, I thought Dr. Carbles might let us skip the after-school march. But he didn't. When the bell rang, he led us out onto the playground and made us march around in the rain. It was horrible.

"Left! Right! Left! Right!" barked Dr. Carbles. "You kids are a disgrace!"

Finally he let us go home. I walked with Ryan and Michael. We were soaked.

"It's not fair!" Ryan said, as we crossed the street next to the school.

"What's not fair?" somebody asked.

It was Mr. Louie, the school crossing guard. He wears bell-bottom pants and tie-dyed shirts, and he always has his guitar with him. Well, actually it's a stop sign. He wrote the word STOP in big letters on the back of his guitar.

We told Mr. Louie all about Dr. Carbles.

"Bummer, man!" Mr. Louie said. "That dude gives off bad vibes."

"And there's nothing we can do about it," Michael said.

"Sure there is!" Mr. Louie told us. "You should protest! That's what they did back in the Sixties, man. It was far-out! Peace and love were in the air. People changed the world by protesting. You can change your world, too!"

It sounded like a great idea. I invited Mr. Louie over to my house after school so he could teach me and the guys how to protest like they did in the Sixties.

Mr. Louie told us that the way to change the world is to sing songs, chant slogans, and hold up signs. Michael made a sign that said POWER TO THE PEOPLE. Ryan made a sign that said DON'T TRUST ANYONE OVER 12. I made a sign that said CARBLES IS LOSING HIS MARBLES!

While we were working on our signs,

Mr. Louie taught us some protest songs, like "Blowin' in the Wind,"**** and "If I Had a Hammer."

I don't get that hammer song. It's about some guy who wants a hammer. Why doesn't he just go to a hardware store and buy one? Hammers don't cost that much. Instead of singing about hammers, I think we should sing "If I Had a Snowboard" or "If I Had an Xbox." That would make a lot more sense than singing about hammers, if you ask me.

Anyway, when me and the guys got to school the next morning, we were ready to protest. We marched around with our

****That's the one that goes, "The ants are my friends, blowin' in the wind."

signs. We chanted slogans. We sang songs. We were in the middle of "If I Had a Snowboard" when Andrea came over to us.

"What are you dumbheads doing?" she asked.

"We're protesting, man!" I said. "We're gonna change the world!"

"You probably don't even change your under-wear, Arlo,"

said Andrea, and she went up the steps to school.

"CARBLES NEVER! KLUTZ FOREVER!" chanted Ryan.

"TWO, FOUR, SIX, EIGHT—WHO DO WE APPRECIATE?" chanted Michael. "KLUTZ! KLUTZ! KLUTZ!"

A bunch of kids gathered around to watch. Some of them joined our protest. A few of the teachers joined in, too. Soon we had a big mob protesting. Everything was going great!

And then, you'll never guess in a million hundred years what came rolling out of the playground.

I'm not going to tell you.

Okay, okay, I'll tell you.

It was a tank!

No, not a fish tank, dumbhead. It was one of those big army tanks. And it was heading our way!

The top of the tank opened up, and Dr. Carbles's head popped out.

"GO TO YOUR CLASSROOMS, NOW!" Dr. Carbles hollered into his bullhorn. "I WILL CRUSH YOUR REBELLION!"

Wow! Where do you think Dr. Carbles got a tank? I guess he rented it. You can rent anything, you know. There's probably a place called Rent-a-Tank.

Dr. Carbles was driving the tank straight at us.

"He wouldn't dare run us over," Michael said.

"GET OUT OF THE WAY!" Dr. Carbles shouted. "OR YOU WILL BE LOCKED IN THE DUNGEON ON THE THIRD FLOOR!"

The tank was getting closer! We didn't know what to say! We didn't know what to do! We had to think fast!

"Run for your lives!" I shouted just as the tank was about to rumble over us.

How to Drive Grown-ups Crazy

Well, that whole protest thing was a dumb idea. Luckily none of us got killed. We'd have to think up another way to get rid of Dr. Carbles.

"Remember how we got rid of Ms. Todd?" Ryan said the next morning while we were putting our backpacks away.

Ms. Todd was a substitute teacher at our school. She tried to murder Miss Daisy and take her job, but we caught her. Ms. Todd was odd.

"Yeah, we drove her crazy," I said.

"Then we have to drive *Dr. Carbles* crazy," said Michael.

If there's one thing I'm good at, it's driving grown-ups crazy. There are lots of ways to do that. One way is to say everything they say right after they say it. That's a good one. Sometimes I ask my parents "Why?" over and over again. It drives them nuts.

But it was Neil the nude kid who had the greatest idea in the history of the world.

"We should steal Dr. Carbles's toupee!" Neil said.

Yeah! Mr. Klutz told us that if anybody ever found out Dr. Carbles was bald, it would drive him crazy! Neil's idea was genius! He should be in the gifted and talented program.

The only problem was, how were we going to steal Dr. Carbles's toupee?

"We could sneak into his house in the middle of the night and rip it off his head," suggested Michael.

"Nah," Ryan said. "He probably has an electric fence and a moat around his house."

"We could rent a giant wind machine and blow it off his head," suggested Michael. "You can rent anything."

"Nah," Ryan said. "It costs a lot of money to rent a giant wind machine."

That's when I got the greatest idea in the history of the world.

"Hey!" I said. "Every day after lunch, Dr. Carbles stands outside and watches us march around the playground, right?"

"Yeah," Michael said. "So what?"

"Well, he has a fishing pole in his office," I told the guys. "We could hang the fishing pole out the second-floor window and go fishing for toupee!"

"You're a genius!" Neil the nude kid

told me.

I should get the No Bell Prize. That's a prize they give out to people who don't have bells.

During lunch me and Neil snuck out of the vomitorium. We slinked around the halls like secret agents. Nobody was around. All the teachers must have been eating in the teachers' lounge.

I opened the door to Dr. Carbles's office. It was empty. Perfect! I grabbed the fishing pole, and we tore out of there.

We ran up the steps to the second floor. I handed Neil the pole and opened a window. We peeked out. Dr. Carbles was right below us, standing there with his bullhorn. The kids were just starting to march out of the vomitorium.

"Left! Right!" Dr. Carbles yelled at the kids. "March, you weasels!"

"This is gonna be great!" Neil giggled as he stuck the fishing pole out the window. "He'll go crazy once we steal his toupee."

"Okay," I told Neil, "drop the hook now."

Neil lowered the line until the hook was hanging right above Dr. Carbles's head.

"A little to the left," I told Neil. "Lower!"

Neil was having a hard time hooking the toupee.

"My arms are getting tired," Neil said.

I grabbed the pole. Neil helped me

guide the hook. It was not easy! The hook kept blowing around.

"Any nibbles yet?" Neil asked.

"Nope." But right after I said that, I felt a little pull on the line. "Hey, I think I got it!"

I started reeling in the toupee, but there was just one problem. It wouldn't come off Dr. Carbles's head! So I pulled harder.

"It's a big one!" I told Neil. "It's a fighter!"

I kept tugging on the fishing pole, but the toupee just wouldn't budge.

"It must be glued on good!" Neil said.

"Maybe they took hair off other parts of his body and planted it on his head," I said. "I saw that on a TV commercial once."

"That's disgusting!" said Neil.

Suddenly Dr. Carbles grabbed his toupee and looked up at us.

"What's the meaning of this!" he shouted.

Uh-oh. I dropped the pole. It fell out the window and almost hit Dr. Carbles on the head.

"A.J., report to my office immediately!" he hollered.

"Ooooooooooooooh!" went all the kids on the playground.

That's it. My life was over. I would have to move to Antarctica and live with the penguins.

The Torture Room

When I got to Dr. Carbles's office, he told me to sit in the chair next to his desk. Then he just stared at me. He looked really mad.

"Are you going to be Frank?" I asked.

He didn't say anything. He pulled down the shades to make the room dark.

Then he turned on his desk lamp and pointed the light on me.

"Who told you I wear a toupee, A.J.?" asked Dr. Carbles. "Huh? Who told you?"

I was pretty sure I had the right to remain silent. I saw that on a TV show once.

Besides, I was too scared to say anything.

"The teachers are plotting against me, aren't they?" Dr. Carbles said. "I don't trust them. I see the way they look at me. They hate me. Everybody hates me."

I kept my mouth shut. If you don't say anything, you can't say anything dumb.

"Did Mr. Docker tell you about my toupee?" asked Dr. Carbles. "Or was it Miss Lazar? You can tell me, A.J."

His face was right next to mine. His breath smelled like rotten eggs. I was shaking. I thought I was gonna die.

"Cat got your tongue, eh?" Dr. Carbles asked. "Well, I have ways to make you talk."

Oh no! He was going to torture me!

"Here, I want you to read this," said Dr. Carbles.

"What is it?" I asked.

"A book."

"A *book*?!" I exclaimed. "With words?"

"That's right," Dr. Carbles said. "Read it."

"Reading is boring," I told him.

"READ IT!" he shouted. "Every word! Cover to cover! Let's go. I don't have all day."

Sweat was rolling down my face.

"No! No!" I cried. "Not reading! Anything but that! Okay, I'll talk! I'll talk!"

"Smart boy," Dr. Carbles said, taking the book away. "I knew you'd see it my way."

"It was Mr. Klutz," I admitted. "I went

over to his house. He told me about your toupee. He told me about the skateboarding team. He told me he called you Walrus Face. He told me *everything.*"

"Klutz, eh?" sneered Dr. Carbles. "Klutz told you that? Oh, I'm going to get him. I'm going to get him good. *Nobody* calls me Walrus Face and gets away with it!"

"Please don't tell Mr. Klutz I told you. I promised him I wouldn't tell. Please, Frank?"

"Get out of here!" Dr. Carbles hollered. "And stop calling me Frank or I'll get the summer reading list!"

I ran out of his office as fast as I could.

The Big Skate-off

When I got to school the next morning, I could hear the sound of hammering. It was coming from the gym. That was weird. I went over to the gym and opened the door. You'll never believe in a million hundred years what I saw.

Five guys in overalls were building a half-pipe! Right there in the gym!

Wow! We were going to go skateboarding in fizz ed!

The fizz ed teacher, Miss Small, is off the wall. She usually has us juggle scarves and balance feathers on our fingers. But we were finally going to do something cool! We were going to skateboard! It was the greatest day of my life.

Me and the guys were so excited, we could hardly stand it.

"When do we go to fizz ed?" we kept asking Miss Daisy.

"I don't know," said Miss Daisy, who doesn't know anything.

Finally, at the end of the day, Mrs. Patty made an announcement over the loudspeaker. She said that everybody had to report to the gym.

"Hooray!" all the boys yelled. Miss Daisy had to keep telling us to stop running the whole way there.

When we got there, the half-pipe was finished, and Dr. Carbles was standing in front of it. He was holding a skateboard.

"Where's Miss Small?" I asked. "Are we going to skateboard in fizz ed?"

"No!" shouted Dr. Carbles. "This half-pipe isn't for you. It's for *me.*"

"Boooooo!" yelled all the boys.

We were really mad as we sat down on the bleachers. But we didn't stay mad for long, because you'll never believe who walked into the door at the other end of the gym.

Nobody. If you walked into a door, it would hurt. But guess who walked into the door*way*?

It was Mr. Klutz! And he was holding a skateboard. Everybody cheered.

"Hooray for Mr. Klutz!" we all shouted.

Dr. Carbles and Mr. Klutz stood facing each other at opposite sides of the gym. They looked like two gunslingers on one of those old Western TV shows, except they had skateboards instead of guns. Everybody got quiet. You could hear a pin drop.

"So, we meet again, Klutz," said Dr. Carbles. "I thought you'd be too chicken to show up."

"I will outskate you *any*time," Mr. Klutz said. "You're going down, Walrus Face!"

"Oh, snap!" Ryan whispered.

"Mr. Klutz is gonna blow the doors off Dr. Carbles!" I told the guys.

Mr. Klutz and Dr. Carbles climbed up to the top of the half-pipe. Dr. Carbles picked up his bullhorn.

"Finally, all the world will know who the best skateboarder is!" he hollered. "Ha-ha-ha! Revenge will be sweet!"

We all started chanting: "TWO, FOUR, SIX, EIGHT—WHO DO WE APPRECIATE? KLUTZ! KLUTZ! KLUTZ!"

Dr. Carbles and Mr. Klutz dropped into the half-pipe at the same time. Dr. Carbles did a vert bomb drop. Mr. Klutz did a combination inward heelflip/outside boardslide. Dr. Carbles did a polejam. Mr. Klutz did a boomerang.

It was awesome! Everybody in the gym was yelling and screaming their heads off. Even the teachers!

Then, just as Dr. Carbles was doing a

monkeyflip jawbreaker, Mr. Klutz did a stalefish McTwist. They crashed into each other in midair! Dr. Carbles's toupee went

flying off his head! The two of them landed together in a tangle of arms and legs. It was a real Kodak moment. And we got to see it live and in person.

"Oh, my leg!" moaned Dr. Carbles.

"Ouch! My head!" moaned Mr. Klutz.

The two of them were lying at the bottom of the half-pipe, freaking out. Mrs. Cooney, the beautiful school nurse, came running over with a first-aid kit. And you'll never believe in a million hundred years who walked in the gym at that exact moment.

I'm not going to tell you.

Okay, okay, I'll tell you.

It was Mrs. Haney, the superintendent

of all the schools in the county!

"Carbles!" she shouted. "What's the meaning of this?"

Dr. Carbles looked at Mr. Klutz. Mr. Klutz looked at Mrs. Haney. Mrs. Haney looked at Dr. Carbles. Everybody was looking at each other.

"It's a half-pipe, ma'am," Dr. Carbles said. "I challenged Klutz to a little competition."

"You were hired to bring order and discipline to this school!" Mrs. Haney yelled. "I didn't bring you here so you could build a half-poop and ride a skateboard!"

"B-b-but . . . ," said Dr. Carbles.

"Carbles!" shouted Mrs. Haney. "You're FIRED!"

Dr. Carbles limped out of the gym, sobbing. What a crybaby!

You Can Rent Anything

"Watch out!" somebody screamed.

It was the day before Thanksgiving. Some crazy lunatic dressed like a Pilgrim was tearing down the sidewalk on a skateboard. He must have built up too much speed. The guy was weaving around kids, totally out of control.

"Run for your lives!" somebody shouted.

The skateboard must have hit a crack in the sidewalk, because the next thing anybody knew, the Pilgrim went flying through the air like a superhero. Kids were diving out of the way. Dogs were running as fast as they could.

The skateboarding Pilgrim crash-landed in the bushes in front of the school. You'll never believe in a million hundred years who it was.

It was Mr. Klutz!

"Good morning, Mr. Klutz," said Mrs. Cooney as she walked past.

"Good morning, Mrs. Cooney," he replied. "Beautiful day, isn't it?"

"Lovely."

Mr. Klutz got up, brushed himself off, and walked up the front steps, like it was totally normal to skateboard to school dressed as a Pilgrim and crash headfirst into the bushes.

Everybody clapped and cheered when

we realized Mr. Klutz had been hired to be our principal again. No more marching. No more uniforms. No more Dr. Carbles. It was the best day in the history of the world.

In the afternoon we were called down to the all-purpose room for an assembly. Mr. Klutz went up on the stage, and everybody gave him a standing ovation.

"Well, I have good news and bad news," Mr. Klutz told us. "The bad news is that even though you all made beautiful Thanksgiving displays, I can't marry a turkey like I promised."

"What happened to Gobbles?" Emily asked.

"I'm having her for dinner tomorrow," Mr. Klutz said.

"What's the good news?" I shouted.

"You'll see." Mr. Klutz went behind the curtain. You'll never believe in a million hundred years what he brought out with him.

A live pig!

"I'm going to marry this pig instead," he told us.

Everybody started cheering and stamping their feet.

"Where did you get a pig?" yelled Ryan.

"From Rent-a-Pig," Mr. Klutz said. "You can rent anything, you know."

Mrs. Roopy came out onstage with a

book. She was wearing a man's suit and tie.

"It's Mrs. Roopy!" everybody yelled.

"I'm not Mrs. Roopy," said Mrs. Roopy. "I'm the justice of the peace. Mr. Klutz, do you take this pig to be your wife—to love, honor, and cherish till death do you part?"

"I do," said Mr. Klutz.

"Pig, do you take Mr. Klutz to be your husband—in sickness and in health, till death do you part?"

"Oink," said the pig.

"This is so romantic!" Andrea whispered.

"I now pronounce you man and wife," said Mrs. Roopy. "Mr. Klutz, you may kiss the pig."

Mr. Klutz bent down and kissed the

pig, right on the lips! Ew, disgusting! That was the second time I saw Mr. Klutz kiss a pig. He must really love pigs.

After the assembly we went back to

Miss Daisy's class to get ready for dismissal. She wished us a Happy Thanksgiving and made us go around in a circle to say what we were thankful for.

"I'm thankful that Mr. Klutz is back," said Andrea.

"I'm thankful that Dr. Carbles is gone," said Michael.

The three-o'clock bell rang.

"What are you thankful for, A.J.?" asked Miss Daisy.

"I'm thankful that we don't have school for four more days," I said. Then I ran out of there.

Maybe Dr. Carbles will take a chill pill

and get his job back. Maybe we'll be allowed to keep the half-pipe and go skateboarding in fizz ed. Maybe Mr. Klutz and the pig will go on a honeymoon and live happily ever after. Maybe Mr. and Mrs. Klutz will get divorced because Mr. Klutz is always kissing pigs and marrying them. Maybe hair will stop growing out of Mr. Klutz's nose and back on the top of his head, where it belongs. Maybe my weird school will become more like a normal school.

But it won't be easy!

Check out the My Weird School series!

#1: Miss Daisy Is Crazy!

The first book in the hilarious series stars A.J., a second grader who hates school—and can't believe his teacher hates it too!

#2: Mr. Klutz Is Nuts!

A.J. can't believe his crazy principal wants to climb to the top of the flagpole!

#3: Mrs. Roopy Is Loopy!

The new librarian thinks she's George Washington one day and Little Bo Peep the next!

#4: Ms. Hannah Is Bananas!

The art teacher wears clothes made from pot holders. Worse than that, she's trying to make A.J. be partners with yucky Andrea!

#5: Miss Small Is off the Wall!

The gym teacher is teaching A.J.'s class to juggle scarves, balance feathers, and do everything *but* play sports!

#6: Mr. Hynde Is Out of His Mind!

The music teacher plays bongo drums on the principal's bald head! But does he have what it takes to be a real rock-and-roll star?

#7: Mrs. Cooney Is Loony!

The school nurse is everybody's favorite—but is she hiding a secret identity?

#8: Ms. LaGrange Is Strange!

The new lunch lady talks funny—and why is she writing secret messages in the mashed potatoes?

#9: Miss Lazar Is Bizarre!

What kind of grown-up *likes* cleaning throw-up? Miss Lazar is the weirdest custodian in the world!

#10: Mr. Docker Is off His Rocker!

The science teacher alarms and amuses A.J.'s class with his wacky experiments and nutty inventions.

#11: Mrs. Kormel Is Not Normal!

A.J.'s school bus gets a flat tire, then becomes hopelessly lost at the hands of the wacky bus driver.

#12: Ms. Todd Is Odd!

Ms. Todd is subbing, and A.J. and his friends are sure she kidnapped Miss Daisy so she could take over her job.

#13: Mrs. Patty Is Batty!

A little bit of spookiness and a lot of humor add up to the best trick-or-treating adventure ever!

#14: Miss Holly Is Too Jolly!

When Miss Holly decks the hall with mistletoe, A.J. knows to watch out. Mistletoe means kissletoe, the worst tradition in the history of the world!

#15: Mr. Macky Is Wacky!

Mr. Macky expects A.J. and his friends to read stuff about the presidents...and even dress up like them! He's taking Presidents' Day way too far!

#16: Ms. Coco Is Loco!

It's Poetry Month and the whole school is poetry crazy, thanks to Ms. Coco. She talks in rhyme! She thinks boys should have feelings! Is she crazy?

#17: Miss Suki Is Kooky!

Miss Suki is a very famous author who writes about endangered animals. But when her pet raptor gets loose during a school visit, it's the kids who are endangered!

#18: Mrs. Yonkers Is Bonkers!

Mrs. Yonkers, the computer teacher, is a nerd who loves anything electronic. She even builds a robot substitute teacher to take her place for a day!

Also look for
#20: Mr. Louie Is Screwy!

When the hippie crossing guard, Mr. Louie, puts a love potion in the water fountain, everyone at Ella Mentry School falls in love! Will A.J. have to kiss Andrea? Yuck!

📖 HarperTrophy®

An Imprint of HarperCollinsPublishers